PENGUIN BOOKS

# Cruelty

Roald Dahl is best known for his mischievous, wildly inventive stories for children. But throughout his life he was also a prolific and acclaimed writer of stories for adults. These sinister, surprising tales continue to entertain, amuse and shock generations of readers even today.

# Cruelty

ROALD DAHL

PENGUIN BOOKS

PENGUIN BOOKS

UK | USA | Canada | Ireland | Australia
India | New Zealand | South Africa

Penguin Books is part of the Penguin Random House group of companies
whose addresses can be found at global.penguinrandomhouse.com.

These stories have been previously published in a variety of publications.
Details of each story's original publication are provided at the start of
each chapter and constitute an extension of this copyright page.
This collection first published in Penguin Books 2016

001

Set in 12.5/14.75pt Garamond MT Std
Typeset by Jouve (UK), Milton Keynes
Printed in Great Britain by Clays Ltd, St Ives plc

A CIP catalogue record for this book is available from the British Library

ISBN: 978-0-718-18565-7

www.greenpenguin.co.uk

# Contents

# The Butler

First published in *Travel and Leisure* (May 1974)
with the title 'The Butler Did It'

As soon as George Cleaver had made his first million, he and Mrs Cleaver moved out of their small suburban villa into an elegant London house. They acquired a French chef called Monsieur Estragon and an English butler called Tibbs, both wildly expensive. With the help of these two experts, the Cleavers set out to climb the social ladder and began to give dinner parties several times a week on a lavish scale.

But these dinners never seemed quite to come off. There was no animation, no spark to set the conversation alight, no style at all. Yet the food was superb and the service faultless.

'What the heck's wrong with our parties, Tibbs?' Mr Cleaver said to the butler. 'Why don't nobody never loosen up and let themselves go?'

Tibbs inclined his head to one side and looked at the ceiling. 'I hope, sir, you will not be offended if I offer a small suggestion.'

'What is it?'

'It's the wine, sir.'

'What about the wine?'

'Well, sir, Monsieur Estragon serves superb food.

Superb food should be accompanied by superb wine. But you serve them a cheap and very odious Spanish red.'

'Then why in heaven's name didn't you say so before, you twit?' cried Mr Cleaver. 'I'm not short of money. I'll give them the best flipping wine in the world if that's what they want! What *is* the best wine in the world?'

'Claret, sir,' the butler replied, 'from the greatest *châteaux* in Bordeaux – Lafite, Latour, Haut-Brion, Margaux, Mouton-Rothschild and Cheval Blanc. And from only the very greatest vintage years, which are, in my opinion, 1906, 1914, 1929 and 1945. Cheval Blanc was also magnificent in 1895 and 1921, and Haut-Brion in 1906.'

'Buy them all!' said Mr Cleaver. 'Fill the flipping cellar from top to bottom!'

'I can try, sir,' the butler said. 'But wines like these are extremely rare and cost a fortune.'

'I don't give a hoot what they cost!' said Mr Cleaver. 'Just go out and get them!'

That was easier said than done. Nowhere in England or in France could Tibbs find any wine from 1895, 1906, 1914 or 1921. But he did manage to get hold of some twenty-nines and forty-fives. The bills for these wines were astronomical. They were in fact so huge that even Mr Cleaver began to sit up and take notice. And his interest quickly turned into outright enthusiasm when the butler suggested to him that a knowledge of wine was a very considerable social asset. Mr Cleaver bought books on the subject and read them from cover to cover. He also learned a great deal from Tibbs himself, who taught him, among other things, just how wine should properly be tasted. 'First, sir, you sniff it long and deep, with your nose right inside the top of the glass, like this. Then you take a mouthful and you open your lips a tiny bit and suck in air, letting the air bubble through the wine. Watch me do it. Then you roll it vigorously around your mouth. And finally you swallow it.'

In due course, Mr Cleaver came to regard himself as an expert on wine, and inevitably he turned into a colossal bore. 'Ladies and gentlemen,' he would announce at dinner, holding up his glass, 'this is a Margaux '29! The greatest year of the century! Fantastic bouquet! Smells of cowslips! And notice especially the after taste and how the tiny trace of tannin gives it that glorious astringent quality! Terrific, ain't it?'

The guests would nod and sip and mumble a few praises, but that was all.

'What's the matter with the silly twerps?' Mr Cleaver said to Tibbs after this had gone on for some time. 'Don't none of them appreciate a great wine?'

The butler laid his head to one side and gazed upward. 'I think they *would* appreciate it, sir,' he said, 'if they were able to taste it. But they can't.'

'What the heck d' you mean, they can't taste it?'

'I believe, sir, that you have instructed Monsieur Estragon to put liberal quantities of vinegar in the salad-dressing.'

'What's wrong with that? I like vinegar.'

'Vinegar,' the butler said, 'is the enemy of wine. It destroys the palate. The dressing should be made of pure olive oil and a little lemon juice. Nothing else.'

'Hogwash!' said Mr Cleaver.

'As you wish, sir.'

'I'll say it again, Tibbs. You're talking hogwash. The vinegar don't spoil my palate one bit.'

'You are very fortunate, sir,' the butler murmured, backing out of the room.

That night at dinner, the host began to mock his butler in front of the guests. 'Mister Tibbs,' he said, 'has been trying to tell me I can't taste my wine if I put vinegar in the salad-dressing. Right, Tibbs?'

'Yes, sir,' Tibbs replied gravely.

'And I told him hogwash. Didn't I, Tibbs?'

'Yes, sir.'

'This wine,' Mr Cleaver went on, raising his glass, 'tastes to me exactly like a Château Lafite '45, and what's more it is a Château Lafite '45.'

Tibbs, the butler, stood very still and erect near the sideboard, his face pale. 'If you'll forgive me, sir,' he said, 'that is not a Lafite '45.'

Mr Cleaver swung round in his chair and stared at the butler. 'What the heck d'you mean,' he said. 'There's the empty bottles beside you to prove it!'

These great clarets, being old and full of sediment, were always decanted by Tibbs before dinner. They were served in cut-glass decanters, while the empty bottles, as is the custom, were placed on the sideboard. Right now, two empty bottles of Lafite '45 were standing on the sideboard for all to see.

'The wine you are drinking, sir,' the butler said quietly, 'happens to be that cheap and rather odious Spanish red.'

Mr Cleaver looked at the wine in his glass, then at the

4

butler. The blood was coming to his face now, his skin was turning scarlet. 'You're lying, Tibbs!' he said.

'No sir, I'm not lying,' the butler said. 'As a matter of fact, I have never served you any other wine but Spanish red since I've been here. It seemed to suit you very well.'

'Don't believe him!' Mr Cleaver cried out to his guests. 'The man's gone mad.'

'Great wines,' the butler said, 'should be treated with reverence. It is bad enough to destroy the palate with three or four cocktails before dinner, as you people do, but when you slosh vinegar over your food into the bargain, then you might just as well be drinking dishwater.'

Ten outraged faces around the table stared at the butler. He had caught them off balance. They were speechless.

'This,' the butler said, reaching out and touching one of the empty bottles lovingly with his fingers, 'this is the last of the forty-fives. The twenty-nines have already been finished. But they were glorious wines. Monsieur Estragon and I enjoyed them immensely.'

The butler bowed and walked quite slowly from the room. He crossed the hall and went out of the front door of the house into the street where Monsieur Estragon was already loading their suitcases into the boot of the small car which they owned together.

# The Great Automatic Grammatizator

First published in *Someone Like You* (1953)

'Well, Knipe, my boy. Now that it's all finished, I just called you in to tell you I think you've done a fine job.'

Adolph Knipe stood still in front of Mr Bohlen's desk. There seemed to be no enthusiasm in him at all.

'Aren't you pleased?'

'Oh yes, Mr Bohlen.'

'Did you see what the papers said this morning?'

'No, sir, I didn't.'

The man behind the desk pulled a folded newspaper towards him, and began to read: 'The building of the great automatic computing engine, ordered by the government some time ago, is now complete. It is probably the fastest electronic calculating machine in the world today. Its function is to satisfy the ever-increasing need of science, industry and administration for rapid mathematical calculation which, in the past, by traditional methods, would have been physically impossible, or would have required more time than the problems justified. The speed with which the new engine works, said Mr John Bohlen, head of the firm of electrical engineers mainly responsible for its construction, may be grasped by the fact that it can provide the correct answer in five seconds to a problem that would occupy a mathematician for a month. In three minutes, it can produce a calculation that by hand (if it were possible) would fill half a million sheets of foolscap paper. The automatic computing engine uses pulses of electricity, generated at the rate of a million a second, to solve all calculations that resolve themselves into addition, subtraction, multiplication and division. For practical purposes there is no limit to what it can do . . .'

Mr Bohlen glanced up at the long, melancholy face of the younger man. 'Aren't you proud, Knipe? Aren't you pleased?'

'Of course, Mr Bohlen.'

'I don't think I have to remind you that your own contribution, especially to the original plans, was an important one. In fact, I might go so far as to say that without you and some of your ideas, this project might still be on the drawing-boards today.'

Adolph Knipe moved his feet on the carpet, and he watched the two small white hands of his chief, the nervous fingers playing with a paper-clip, unbending it, straightening out the hairpin curves. He didn't like the man's hands. He didn't like his face either, with the tiny mouth and the narrow purple-coloured lips. It was unpleasant the way only the lower lip moved when he talked.

'Is anything bothering you, Knipe? Anything on your mind?'

'Oh no, Mr Bohlen. No.'

'How would you like to take a week's holiday? Do you good. You've earned it.'

'Oh, I don't know, sir.'

The older man waited, watching this tall, thin person who stood so sloppily before him. He was a difficult boy.

7

Why couldn't he stand up straight? Always drooping and untidy, with spots on his jacket, and hair falling all over his face.

'I'd like you to take a holiday, Knipe. You need it.'

'All right, sir. If you wish.'

'Take a week. Two weeks if you like. Go somewhere warm. Get some sunshine. Swim. Relax. Sleep. Then come back, and we'll have another talk about the future.'

Adolph Knipe went home by bus to his two-room apartment. He threw his coat on the sofa, poured himself a drink of whisky, and sat down in front of the typewriter that was on the table. Mr Bohlen was right. Of course he was right. Except that he didn't know the half of it. He probably thought it was a woman. Whenever a young man gets depressed, everybody thinks it's a woman.

He leaned forward and began to read through the half-finished sheet of typing still in the machine. It was headed 'A Narrow Escape', and it began: *'The night was dark and stormy, the wind whistled in the trees, the rain poured down like cats and dogs . . .'*

Adolph Knipe took a sip of whisky, tasting the malty-bitter flavour, feeling the trickle of cold liquid as it travelled down his throat and settled in the top of his stomach, cool at first, then spreading and becoming warm, making a little area of warmness in the gut. To hell with Mr John Bohlen anyway. And to hell with the great electrical computing machine. To hell with . . .

At exactly that moment, his eyes and mouth began slowly to open, in a sort of wonder, and slowly he raised his head and became still, absolutely motionless, gazing at the wall opposite with this look that was more perhaps of astonishment than of wonder, but quite fixed now, unmoving, and remaining thus for forty, fifty, sixty seconds. Then gradually (the head still motionless), a subtle change spreading over the face, astonishment becoming pleasure, very slight at first, only around the corners of the mouth, increasing gradually, spreading out until at last the whole face was open wide and shining with extreme delight. It was the first time Adolph Knipe had smiled in many, many months.

'Of course,' he said, speaking aloud, 'it's completely ridiculous.' Again he smiled, raising his upper lip and baring his teeth in a queerly sensual manner.

'It's a delicious idea, but so impracticable it doesn't really bear thinking about at all.'

From then on, Adolph Knipe began to think about nothing else. The idea fascinated him enormously, at first because it gave him a promise – however remote – of revenging himself in a most devilish manner upon his greatest enemies. From this angle alone, he toyed idly with it for perhaps ten or fifteen minutes; then all at once he found himself examining it quite seriously as a practical possibility. He took paper and made some preliminary notes. But he didn't get far. He found himself, almost immediately, up against the old truth that a machine, however ingenious, is incapable of original thought. It can handle no problems except those that resolve themselves into mathematical terms – problems that contain one, and only one, correct answer.

This was a stumper. There didn't seem any way around

it. A machine cannot have a brain. On the other hand, it *can* have a memory, can it not? Their own electronic calculator had a marvellous memory. Simply by converting electric pulses, through a column of mercury, into supersonic waves, it could store away at least a thousand numbers at a time, extracting any one of them at the precise moment it was needed. Would it not be possible, therefore, on this principle, to build a memory section of almost unlimited size?

Now what about that?

Then suddenly, he was struck by a powerful but simple little truth, and it was this: *That English grammar is governed by rules that are almost mathematical in their strictness!* Given the words, and given the sense of what is to be said, then there is only one correct order in which those words can be arranged.

No, he thought, that isn't quite accurate. In many sentences there are several alternative positions for words and phrases, all of which may be grammatically correct. But what the hell. The theory itself is basically true. Therefore, it stands to reason that an engine built along the lines of the electric computer could be adjusted to arrange words (instead of numbers) in their right order according to the rules of grammar. Give it the verbs, the nouns, the adjectives, the pronouns, store them in the memory section as a vocabulary, and arrange for them to be extracted as required. Then feed it with plots and leave it to write the sentences.

There was no stopping Knipe now. He went to work immediately, and there followed during the next few days a period of intense labour. The living-room became littered with sheets of paper: formulae and calculations; lists of words, thousands and thousands of words; the plots of stories, curiously broken up and subdivided; huge extracts from *Roget's Thesaurus*; pages filled with the first names of men and women; hundreds of surnames taken from the telephone directory; intricate drawings of wires and circuits and switches and thermionic valves; drawings of machines that could punch holes of different shapes in little cards, and of a strange electric typewriter that could type ten thousands words a minute. Also a kind of control panel with a series of small push-buttons, each one labelled with the name of a famous American magazine.

He was working in a mood of exultation, prowling around the room amidst this littering of paper, rubbing his hands together, talking out loud to himself; and sometimes, with a sly curl of the nose he would mutter a series of murderous imprecations in which the word 'editor' seemed always to be present. On the fifteenth day of continuous work, he collected the papers into two large folders which he carried – almost at a run – to the offices of John Bohlen Inc., electrical engineers.

Mr Bohlen was pleased to see him back.

'Well, Knipe, good gracious me, you look a hundred per cent better. You have a good holiday? Where'd you go?'

He's just as ugly and untidy as ever, Mr Bohlen thought. Why doesn't he stand up straight? He looks like a bent stick. 'You look a hundred per cent better, my boy.' I wonder what he's grinning about. Every time I see him, his ears seem to have got larger.

Adolph Knipe placed the folders on the desk. 'Look, Mr Bohlen!' he cried. 'Look at these!'

Then he poured out his story. He opened the folders and pushed the plans in front of the astonished little man. He talked for over an hour, explaining everything, and when he had finished, he stepped back, breathless, flushed, waiting for the verdict.

'You know what I think, Knipe? I think you're nuts.' Careful now, Mr Bohlen told himself. Treat him carefully. He's valuable, this one is. If only he didn't look so awful, with that long horse face and the big teeth. The fellow had ears as big as rhubarb leaves.

'But Mr Bohlen! It'll work! I've proved to you it'll work! You can't deny that!'

'Take it easy now, Knipe. Take it easy, and listen to me.'

Adolph Knipe watched his man, disliking him more every second.

'This idea,' Mr Bohlen's lower lip was saying, 'is very ingenious – I might almost say brilliant – and it only goes to confirm my opinion of your abilities, Knipe. But don't take it too seriously. After all, my boy, what possible use can it be to us? Who on earth wants a machine for writing stories? And where's the money in it, anyway? Just tell me that.'

'May I sit down, sir?'

'Sure, take a seat.'

Adolph Knipe seated himself on the edge of a chair. The older man watched him with alert brown eyes, wondering what was coming now.

'I would like to explain something, Mr Bohlen, if I may, about how I came to do all this.'

'Go right ahead, Knipe.' He would have to be humoured a little now, Mr Bohlen told himself. The boy was really valuable – a sort of genius, almost – worth his weight in gold to the firm. Just look at these papers here. Darndest thing you ever saw. Astonishing piece of work. Quite useless, of course. No commercial value. But it proved again the boy's ability.

'It's a sort of confession, I suppose, Mr Bohlen. I think it explains why I've always been so . . . so kind of worried.'

'You tell me anything you want, Knipe. I'm here to help you – you know that.'

The young man clasped his hands together tight on his lap, hugging himself with his elbows. It seemed as though suddenly he was feeling very cold.

'You see, Mr Bohlen, to tell the honest truth, I don't really care much for my work here. I know I'm good at it and all that sort of thing, but my heart's not in it. It's not what I want to do most.'

Up went Mr Bohlen's eyebrows, quick like a spring. His whole body became very still.

'You see, sir, all my life I've wanted to be a writer.'

'A writer!'

'Yes, Mr Bohlen. You may not believe it, but every bit of spare time I've had, I've spent writing stories. In the last ten years I've written hundreds, literally hundreds of short stories. Five hundred and sixty-six, to be precise. Approximately one a week.'

'Good heavens, man! What on earth did you do that for?'

'All I know, sir, is I have the urge.'

'What sort of urge?'

'The creative urge, Mr Bohlen.' Every time he looked up he saw Mr Bohlen's lips. They were growing thinner and thinner, more and more purple.

'And may I ask you what you do with these stories, Knipe?'

'Well, sir, that's the trouble. No one will buy them. Each time I finish one, I send it out on the rounds. It goes to one magazine after another. That's all that happens, Mr Bohlen, and they simply send them back. It's very depressing.'

Mr Bohlen relaxed. 'I can see quite well how you feel, my boy.' His voice was dripping with sympathy. 'We all go through it one time or another in our lives. But now – now that you've had proof – positive proof – from the experts themselves, from the editors, that your stories are – what shall I say – rather unsuccessful, it's time to leave off. Forget it, my boy. Just forget all about it.'

'No, Mr Bohlen! No! That's not true! I *know* my stories are good. My heavens, when you compare them with the stuff some of those magazines print – oh my word, Mr Bohlen! – the sloppy, boring stuff that you see in the magazines week after week – why, it drives me mad!'

'Now wait a minute, my boy . . .'

'Do you ever read the magazines, Mr Bohlen?'

'You'll pardon me, Knipe, but what's all this got to do with your machine?'

'Everything, Mr Bohlen, absolutely everything! What I want to tell you is, I've made a study of magazines, and it seems that each one tends to have its own particular type of story. The writers – the successful ones – know this, and they write accordingly.'

'Just a minute, my boy. Calm yourself down, will you. I don't think all this is getting us anywhere.'

'*Please*, Mr Bohlen, hear me through. It's all terribly important.' He paused to catch his breath. He was properly worked up now, throwing his hands around as he talked. The long, toothy face, with the big ears on either side, simply shone with enthusiasm, and there was an excess of saliva in his mouth which caused him to speak his words wet. 'So you see, on my machine, by having an adjustable co-ordinator between the "plot-memory" section and the "word-memory" section I am able to produce any type of story I desire simply by pressing the required button.'

'Yes, I know, Knipe, I know. This is all very interesting, but what's the point of it?'

'Just this, Mr Bohlen. The market is limited. We've got to be able to produce the right stuff, at the right time, whenever we want it. It's a matter of business, that's all. I'm looking at it from *your* point of view now – as a commercial proposition.'

'My dear boy, it can't possibly be a commercial proposition – ever. You know as well as I do what it costs to build one of these machines.'

'Yes, sir, I do. But with due respect, I don't believe you know what the magazines pay writers for stories.'

'What do they pay?'

'Anything up to twenty-five hundred dollars. It probably averages around a thousand.'

Mr Bohlen jumped.

'Yes, *sir*, it's true.'

'Absolutely impossible, Knipe! Ridiculous!'

'No, sir, it's true.'

'You mean to sit there and tell me that these magazines pay out money like that to a man for . . . just for scribbling off a story! Good heavens, Knipe! Whatever next! Writers must all be millionaires!'

'That's exactly it, Mr Bohlen! That's where the machine comes in. Listen a minute, sir, while I tell you some more. I've got it all worked out. The big magazines are carrying approximately three fiction stories in each issue. Now, take the fifteen most important magazines – the ones paying the most money. A few of them are monthlies, but most of them come out every week. All right. That makes, let us say, around forty big stories being bought each week. That's forty thousand dollars. So with our machine – when we get it working properly – we can collar nearly the whole of this market!'

'My dear boy, you're mad!'

'No, sir, honestly, it's true what I say. Don't you see that with volume alone we'll completely overwhelm them! This machine can produce a five-thousand word story, all typed and ready for dispatch, in thirty seconds. How can the writers compete with that? I ask you, Mr Bohlen, *how?*'

At that point, Adolph Knipe noticed a slight change in the man's expression, an extra brightness in the eyes, the nostrils distending, the whole face becoming still, almost rigid. Quickly, he continued. 'Nowadays, Mr Bohlen, the hand-made article hasn't a hope. It can't possibly compete with mass-production, especially in this country – you know that. Carpets ... chairs ... shoes ... bricks ... crockery ... anything you like to mention – they're all made by machinery now. The quality may be inferior, but that doesn't matter. It's the cost of production that counts. And stories – well – they're just another product, like carpets and chairs, and no one cares how you produce them so long as you deliver the goods. We'll sell them whole-sale, Mr Bohlen! We'll undercut every writer in the country! We'll corner the market!'

Mr Bohlen edged up straighter in his chair. He was leaning forward now, both elbows on the desk, the face alert, the small brown eyes resting on the speaker.

'I still think it's impracticable, Knipe.'

'Forty thousand a week!' cried Adolph Knipe. 'And if we halve the price, making it twenty thousand a week, that's still a million a year!' And softly he added, 'You didn't get any million a year for building the old electronic calculator, did you, Mr Bohlen?'

'But seriously now, Knipe. D'you really think they'd buy them?'

'Listen, Mr Bohlen. Who on earth is going to want custom-made stories when they can get the other kind at half the price? It stands to reason, doesn't it?'

'And how will you sell them? Who will you say has writ-ten them?'

'We'll set up our own literary agency, and we'll distrib-ute them through that. And we'll invent all the names we want for the writers.'

'I don't like it, Knipe. To me, that smacks of trickery, does it not?'

'And another thing, Mr Bohlen. There's all manner of valuable by-products once you've got started. Take advertising, for example. Beer manufacturers and people like that are willing to pay good money these days if famous writers will lend their names to their products. Why, my heavens, Mr Bohlen! This isn't any children's plaything we're talking about. It's big business.'

'Don't get too ambitious, my boy.'

'And another thing. There isn't any reason why we shouldn't put *your* name, Mr Bohlen, on some of the better stories, if you wished it.'

'My goodness, Knipe. What should I want that for?'

'I don't know, sir, except that some writers get to be very much respected – like Mr Erle Gardner or Kathleen Norris, for example. We've got to have names, and I was certainly thinking of using my own on one or two stories, just to help out.'

'A writer, eh?' Mr Bohlen said, musing. 'Well, it would surely surprise them over at the club when they saw my name in the magazines – the good magazines.'

'That's right, Mr Bohlen.'

For a moment, a dreamy, faraway look came into Mr Bohlen's eyes, and he smiled. Then he stirred himself and began leafing through the plans that lay before him.

'One thing I don't quite understand, Knipe. Where do the plots come from? The machine can't possibly invent plots.'

'We feed those in, sir. That's no problem at all. Everyone has plots. There's three or four hundred of them written down in that folder there on your left. Feed them straight into the "plot-memory" section of the machine.'

'Go on.'

'There are many other little refinements too, Mr Bohlen. You'll see them all when you study the plans carefully. For example, there's a trick that nearly every writer uses, of inserting at least one long, obscure word into each story. This makes the reader think that the man is very wise and clever. So I have the machine do the same thing. There'll be a whole stack of long words stored away just for this purpose.'

'Where?'

'In the "word-memory" section,' he said, epexegetic-ally.

Through most of that day the two men discussed the possibilities of the new engine. In the end, Mr Bohlen said he would have to think about it some more. The next morning, he was quietly enthusiastic. Within a week, he was completely sold on the idea.

'What we'll have to do, Knipe, is to say that we're merely building another mathematical calculator, but of a new type. That'll keep the secret.'

'Exactly, Mr Bohlen.'

And in six months the machine was completed. It was housed in a separate brick building at the back of the premises, and now that it was ready for action, no one was allowed near it excepting Mr Bohlen and Adolph Knipe.

It was an exciting moment when the two men – the one,

short, plump, breviped – the other tall, thin and toothy – stood in the corridor before the control panel and got ready to run off the first story. All around them were walls dividing up into many small corridors, and the walls were covered with wiring and plugs and switches and huge glass valves. They were both nervous, Mr Bohlen hopping from one foot to the other, quite unable to keep still.

'Which button?' Adolph Knipe asked, eyeing a row of small white discs that resembled the keys of a typewriter. 'You choose, Mr Bohlen. Lots of magazines to pick from – *Saturday Evening Post, Collier's, Ladies' Home Journal* – any one you like.'

'Goodness me, boy! How do I know?' He was jumping up and down like a man with hives.

'Mr Bohlen,' Adolph Knipe said gravely, 'do you realize that at this moment, with your little finger alone, you have it in your power to become the most versatile writer on this continent?'

'Listen, Knipe, just get on with it, will you please – and cut out the preliminaries.'

'OK, Mr Bohlen. Then we'll make it . . . let me see – this one. How's that?' He extended one finger and pressed down a button with the name TODAY'S WOMAN printed across it in diminutive black type. There was a sharp click, and when he took his finger away, the button remained down, below the level of the others.

'So much for the selection,' he said. 'Now – here we go!' He reached up and pulled a switch on the panel. Immediately, the room was filled with a loud humming noise, and a crackling of electric sparks, and the jingle of many, tiny, quickly moving levers; and almost in the same instant, sheets of quarto paper began sliding out from a slot to the right of the control panel and dropping into a basket below. They came out quick, one sheet a second, and in less than half a minute it was all over. The sheets stopped coming.

'That's it!' Adolph Knipe cried. 'There's your story!'

They grabbed the sheets and began to read. The first one they picked up started as follows: 'Aifkjmbsaoeg weztpplnvoqudskigt&,fuhpekanvbertyuiolkjhgfdsazxcvb nm,peruitrehdjkgmvnb,wmsuy . . .' They looked at the others. The style was roughly similar in all of them. Mr Bohlen began to shout. The younger man tried to calm him down.

'It's all right, sir. Really it is. It only needs a little adjustment. We've got a connection wrong somewhere, that's all. You must remember, Mr Bohlen, there's over a million feet of wiring in this room. You can't expect everything to be right first time.'

'It'll never work,' Mr Bohlen said.

'Be patient, sir. Be patient.'

Adolph Knipe set out to discover the fault, and in four days' time he announced that all was ready for the next try.

'It'll never work,' Mr Bohlen said. 'I know it'll never work.'

Knipe smiled and pressed the selector button marked *Reader's Digest*. Then he pulled the switch, and again the strange, exciting, humming sound filled the room. One page of typescript flew out of the slot into the basket.

'Where's the rest?' Mr Bohlen cried. 'It's stopped! It's gone wrong!'

'No, sir, it hasn't. It's exactly right. It's for the *Digest*, don't you see?'

This time it began: 'Fewpeopleyetknowthatarevolu tionarynewcurehasbeendiscoveredwhichmaywellbringper manentrelieftosufferersofthemostdreadeddiseaseofour time . . .' And so on.

'It's gibberish!' Mr Bohlen shouted.

'No, sir, it's fine. Can't you see? It's simply that she's not breaking up the words. That's an easy adjustment. But the story's there. Look, Mr Bohlen, look! It's all there except that the words are joined together.'

And indeed it was.

On the next try a few days later, everything was perfect, even the punctuation. The first story they ran off, for a famous women's magazine, was a solid, plotty story of a boy who wanted to better himself with his rich employer. This boy arranged, so the story went, for a friend to hold up the rich man's daughter on a dark night when she was driving home. Then the boy himself, happening by, knocked the gun out of his friend's hand and rescued the girl. The girl was grateful. But the father was suspicious. He questioned the boy sharply. The boy broke down and confessed. Then the father, instead of kicking him out of the house, said that he admired the boy's resourcefulness. The girl admired his honesty – and his looks. The father promised him to be head of the Accounts Department. The girl married him.

'It's tremendous, Mr Bohlen! It's exactly right!'

'Seems a bit sloppy to me, my boy.'

'No, sir, it's a seller, a real seller!'

In his excitement, Adolph Knipe promptly ran off six more stories in as many minutes. All of them – except one, which for some reason came out a trifle lewd – seemed entirely satisfactory.

Mr Bohlen was now mollified. He agreed to set up a literary agency in an office downtown, and to put Knipe in charge. In a couple of weeks, this was accomplished. Then Knipe mailed out the first dozen stories. He put his own name to four of them, Mr Bohlen's to one, and for the others he simply invented names.

Five of these stories were promptly accepted. The one with Mr Bohlen's name on it was turned down with a letter from the fiction editor saying, 'This is a skilful job, but in our opinion it doesn't quite come off. We would like to see more of this writer's work . . .' Adolph Knipe took a cab out to the factory and ran off another story for the same magazine. He again put Mr Bohlen's name to it, and mailed it immediately. That one they bought.

The money started pouring in. Knipe slowly and carefully stepped up the output, and in six months' time he was delivering thirty stories a week, and selling about half.

He began to make a name for himself in literary circles as a prolific and successful writer. So did Mr Bohlen; but not quite such a good name, although he didn't know it. At the same time, Knipe was building up a dozen or more fictitious persons as promising young authors. Everything was going fine.

At this point it was decided to adapt the machine for

writing novels as well as stories. Mr Bohlen, thirsting now for greater honours in the literary world, insisted that Knipe go to work at once on this prodigious task.

'I want to do a novel,' he kept saying. 'I want to do a novel.'

'And so you will, sir. And so you will. But please be patient. This is a very complicated adjustment I have to make.'

'Everyone tells me I ought to do a novel,' Mr Bohlen cried. 'All sorts of publishers are chasing after me day and night begging me to stop fooling around with stories and do something really important instead. A novel's the only thing that counts – that's what they say.'

'We're going to do novels,' Knipe told him. 'Just as many as we want. But please be patient.'

'Now listen to me, Knipe. What I'm going to do is a *serious* novel, something that'll make 'em sit up and take notice. I've been getting rather tired of the sort of stories you've been putting my name to lately. As a matter of fact, I'm none too sure you haven't been trying to make a monkey out of me.'

'A monkey, Mr Bohlen?'

'Keeping all the best ones for yourself, that's what you've been doing.'

'Oh no, Mr Bohlen! No!'

'So this time I'm going to make damn sure I write a high-class intelligent book. You understand that.'

'Look, Mr Bohlen. With the sort of switchboard I'm rigging up, you'll be able to write any sort of book you want.'

And this was true, for within another couple of months, the genius of Adolph Knipe had not only adapted the machine for novel writing, but had constructed a marvellous new control system which enabled the author to pre-select literally any type of plot and any style of writing he desired. There were so many dials and levers on the thing, it looked like the instrument panel of some enormous aeroplane.

First, by depressing one of a series of master buttons, the writer made his primary decision: historical, satirical, philosophical, political, romantic, erotic, humorous or straight. Then, from the second row (the basic buttons), he chose his theme: army life, pioneer days, civil war, world war, racial problem, wild west, country life, childhood memories, seafaring, the sea bottom and many, many more. The third row of buttons gave a choice of literary style: classical, whimsical, racy, Hemingway, Faulkner, Joyce, feminine, etc. The fourth row was for characters, the fifth for wordage – and so on and so on – ten long rows of pre-selector buttons.

But that wasn't all. Control had also to be exercised during the actual writing process (which took about fifteen minutes per novel), and to do this the author had to sit, as it were, in the driver's seat, and pull (or push) a battery of labelled stops, as on an organ. By so doing, he was able continually to modulate or merge fifty different and variable qualities such as tension, surprise, humour, pathos and mystery. Numerous dials and gauges on the dashboard itself told him throughout exactly how far along he was with his work.

Finally, there was the question of 'passion'. From a careful study of the books at the top of the best-seller lists for the past year, Adolph Knipe had decided that this was the most important ingredient of all – a magical catalyst that somehow or other could transform the dullest novel into a howling success – at any rate financially. But Knipe also knew that passion was powerful, heady stuff, and must be prudently dispensed – the right proportions at the right moments; and to ensure this, he had devised an independent control consisting of two sensitive sliding adjustors operated by foot-pedals, similar to the throttle and brake in a car. One pedal governed the percentage of passion to be injected, the other regulated its intensity. There was no doubt, of course – and this was the only drawback – that the writing of a novel by the Knipe methods was going to be rather like flying a plane and driving a car and playing an organ all at the same time, but this did not trouble the inventor. When all was ready, he proudly escorted Mr Bohlen into the machine house and began to explain the operating procedure for the new wonder.

'Good God, Knipe! I'll never be able to do all that! Dammit, man, it'd be easier to write the thing by hand!'

'You'll soon get used to it, Mr Bohlen, I promise you. In a week or two, you'll be doing it without hardly thinking. It's just like learning to drive.'

Well, it wasn't quite as easy at that, but after many hours of practice, Mr Bohlen began to get the hang of it, and finally, late one evening, he told Knipe to make ready for running off the first novel. It was a tense moment, with the fat little man crouching nervously in the driver's seat, and the tall toothy Knipe fussing excitedly around him.

'I intend to write an important novel, Knipe.'

'I'm sure you will, sir. I'm sure you will.'

With one finger, Mr Bohlen carefully pressed the necessary pre-selector buttons:

Master button – *satirical*

Subject – *racial problem*

Style – *classical*

Characters – *six men, four women, one infant*

Length – *fifteen chapters*

At the same time he had his eye particularly upon three organ stops marked *power, mystery, profundity*.

'Are you ready, sir?'

'Yes, yes, I'm ready.'

Knipe pulled the switch. The great engine hummed. There was a deep whirring sound from the oiled movement of fifty thousand cogs and rods and levers; then came the drumming of the rapid electrical typewriter, setting up a shrill, almost intolerable clatter. Out into the basket flew the typewritten pages – one every two seconds. But what with the noise and the excitement, and having to play upon the stops, and watch the chapter-counter and the pace-indicator and the passion-gauge, Mr Bohlen began to panic. He reacted in precisely the way a learner driver does in a car – by pressing both feet hard down on the pedals and keeping them there until the thing stopped.

'Congratulations on your first novel,' Knipe said, picking up the great bundle of typed pages from the basket.

Little pearls of sweat were oozing out all over Mr Bohlen's face. 'It sure was hard work, my boy.'

'But you got it done, sir. You got it done.'

'Let me see it, Knipe. How does it read?'

He started to go through the first chapter, passing each finished page to the younger man.

'Good heavens, Knipe! What's this!' Mr Bohlen's thin purple fish-lip was moving slightly as it mouthed the words, his cheeks were beginning slowly to inflate.

'But look here, Knipe! This is outrageous!'

'I must say it's a bit fruity, sir.'

'*Fruity!* It's perfectly revolting! I can't possibly put my name to this!'

'Quite right, sir. Quite right.'

'Knipe! Is this some nasty trick you've been playing on me?'

'Oh no, sir! No!'

'It certainly looks like it.'

'You don't think, Mr Bohlen, that you mightn't have been pressing a little hard on the passion-control pedals, do you?'

'My dear boy, how should *I* know.'

'Why don't you try another?'

So Mr Bohlen ran off a second novel, and this time it went according to plan.

Within a week, the manuscript had been read and accepted by an enthusiastic publisher. Knipe followed with one in his own name, then made a dozen more for good measure. In no time at all, Adolph Knipe's Literary Agency had become famous for its large stable of promising young novelists. And once again the money started rolling in.

It was at this stage that young Knipe began to display a real talent for big business.

'See here, Mr Bohlen,' he said. 'We still got too much competition. Why don't we just absorb all the other writers in the country?'

Mr Bohlen, who now sported a bottle-green velvet jacket and allowed his hair to cover two-thirds of his ears, was quite content with things the way they were. 'Don't know what you mean, my boy. You can't just absorb writers.'

'Of course you can, sir. Exactly like Rockefeller did with his oil companies. Simply buy 'em out, and if they won't sell, squeeze 'em out. It's easy!'

'Careful now, Knipe. Be careful.'

'I've got a list here, sir, of fifty of the most successful writers in the country, and what I intend to do is offer each one of them a lifetime contract with pay. All *they* have to do is undertake never to write another word; and, of course, to let us use their names on our own stuff. How about that.'

'They'll never agree.'

'You don't know writers, Mr Bohlen. You watch and see.'

'What about the creative urge, Knipe?'

'It's bunk! All they're really interested in is the money – just like everybody else.'

In the end, Mr Bohlen reluctantly agreed to give it a try, and Knipe, with his list of writers in his pocket, went off in a large chauffeur-driven Cadillac to make his calls.

He journeyed first to the man at the top of the list, a very great and wonderful writer, and he had no trouble getting into the house. He told his story and produced a suitcase full of sample novels, and a contract for the man to sign which guaranteed him so much a year for life. The man listened politely, decided he was dealing with a lunatic, gave him a drink, then firmly showed him to the door.

The second writer on the list, when he saw Knipe was serious, actually attacked him with a large metal paperweight, and the inventor had to flee down the garden followed by such a torrent of abuse and obscenity as he had never heard before.

But it took more than this to discourage Adolph Knipe. He was disappointed but not dismayed, and off he went in his big car to seek his next client. This one was a female, famous and popular, whose fat romantic books sold by the million across the country. She received Knipe graciously, gave him tea and listened attentively to his story.

'It all sounds very fascinating,' she said. 'But of course I find it a little hard to believe.'

'Madam,' Knipe answered. 'Come with me and see it with your own eyes. My car awaits you.'

So off they went, and in due course, the astonished lady was ushered into the machine house where the wonder was kept. Eagerly, Knipe explained its workings, and after a while he even permitted her to sit in the driver's seat and practise with the buttons.

'All right,' he said suddenly, 'you want to do a book now?'

'Oh yes!' she cried. 'Please!'

She was very competent and seemed to know exactly what she wanted. She made her own pre-selections, then ran off a long, romantic, passion-filled novel. She read through the first chapter and became so enthusiastic that she signed up on the spot.

'That's one of them out of the way,' Knipe said to Mr Bohlen afterwards. 'A pretty big one too.'

'Nice work, my boy.'

'And you know *why* she signed?'

'Why?'

'It wasn't the money. She's got plenty of that.'

'Then why?'

Knipe grinned, lifting his lip and baring a long pale upper gum. 'Simply because she saw the machine-made stuff was better than her own.'

Thereafter, Knipe wisely decided to concentrate only upon mediocrity. Anything better than that – and there were so few it didn't matter much – was apparently not quite so easy to seduce.

In the end, after several months of work, he had persuaded something like seventy per cent of the writers on his list to sign the contract. He found that the older ones, those who were running out of ideas and had taken to drink, were the easiest to handle. The younger people were more troublesome. They were apt to become abusive, sometimes violent when he approached them; and more than once Knipe was slightly injured on his rounds.

But on the whole, it was a satisfactory beginning. This last year – the first full year of the machine's operation – it was estimated that at least one half of all the novels and stories published in the English language were produced by Adolph Knipe upon the Great Automatic Grammatizator.

Does this surprise you?

I doubt it.

And worse is yet to come. Today, as the secret spreads, many more are hurrying to tie up with Mr Knipe. And all the time the screw turns tighter for those who hesitate to sign their names.

This very moment, as I sit here listening to the howling of my nine starving children in the other room, I can feel my own hand creeping closer and closer to that golden contract that lies over on the other side of the desk.

Give us strength, oh Lord, to let our children starve.

# Royal Jelly

First published in *Kiss Kiss* (1960)

'It worries me to death, Albert, it really does,' Mrs Taylor said.

She kept her eyes fixed on the baby who was now lying absolutely motionless in the crook of her left arm.

'I just know there's something wrong.'

The skin on the baby's face had a pearly translucent quality, and was stretched very tightly over the bones.

'Try again,' Albert Taylor said.

'It won't do any good.'

'You have to keep trying, Mabel,' he said.

She lifted the bottle out of the saucepan of hot water and shook a few drops of milk on to the inside of her wrist, testing for temperature.

'Come on,' she whispered. 'Come on, my baby. Wake up and take a bit more of this.'

There was a small lamp on the table close by that made a soft yellow glow all around her.

'Please,' she said. 'Take just a weeny bit more.'

The husband watched her over the top of his magazine. She was half dead with exhaustion, he could see that, and the pale oval face, usually so grave and serene, had taken on a kind of pinched and desperate look. But even so, the drop of her head as she gazed down at the child was curiously beautiful.

'You see,' she murmured. 'It's no good. She won't have it.'

She held the bottle up to the light, squinting at the calibrations.

'One ounce again. That's all she's taken. No – it isn't even that. It's only three quarters. It's not enough to keep body and soul together, Albert, it really isn't. It worries me to death.'

'I know,' he said.

'If only they could *find out* what was wrong.'

'There's nothing wrong, Mabel. It's just a matter of time.'

'Of course there's something wrong.'

'Dr Robinson says no.'

'Look,' she said, standing up. 'You can't tell me it's natural for a six-weeks-old child to weigh less, less by more than *two whole pounds* than she did when she was born! Just look at those legs! They're nothing but skin and bone!'

The tiny baby lay limply on her arm, not moving.

'Dr Robinson said you was to stop worrying, Mabel. So did that other one.'

'Ha!' she said. 'Isn't that wonderful! I'm to stop worrying!'

'Now, Mabel.'

'What does he want me to do? Treat it as some sort of a joke?'

'He didn't say that.'

'I hate doctors! I hate them all!' she cried, and she swung away from him and walked quickly out of the room towards the stairs, carrying the baby with her.

Albert Taylor stayed where he was and let her go.

In a little while he heard her moving about in the bedroom directly over his head, quick nervous footsteps going tap tap tap on the linoleum above. Soon the footsteps would stop, and then he would have to get up and follow her, and when he went into the bedroom he would find her sitting beside the cot as usual, staring at the child and crying softly to herself and refusing to move.

'She's starving, Albert,' she would say.

'Of course she's not starving.'

'She *is* starving. I know she is. And Albert?'

'Yes?'

'I believe you know it too, but you won't admit it. Isn't that right?'

Every night now it was like this.

Last week they had taken the child back to the hospital, and the doctor had examined it carefully and told them that there was nothing the matter.

'It took us nine years to get this baby, Doctor,' Mabel had said. 'I think it would kill me if anything should happen to her.'

That was six days ago and since then it had lost another five ounces.

But worrying about it wasn't going to help anybody, Albert Taylor told himself. One simply had to trust the doctor on a thing like this. He picked up the magazine that was still lying on his lap and glanced idly down the list of contents to see what it had to offer this week:

All his life Albert Taylor had been fascinated by anything that had to do with bees. As a small boy he used often to catch them in his bare hands and go running with them into the house to show to his mother, and sometimes he would put them on his face and let them crawl about over his cheeks and neck, and the astonishing thing about it all was that he never got stung. On the contrary, the bees seemed to enjoy being with him. They never tried to fly away, and to get rid of them he would have to brush them off gently with his fingers. Even then they would frequently return and settle again on his arm or hand or knee, any place where the skin was bare.

His father, who was a bricklayer, said there must be some witch's stench about the boy, something noxious that came oozing out through the pores of the skin, and that no good would ever come of it, hypnotizing insects like that. But the mother said it was a gift given him by God, and even went so far as to compare him with St Francis and the birds.

As he grew older, Albert Taylor's fascination with bees developed into an obsession, and by the time he was twelve he had built his first hive. The following summer he had captured his first swarm. Two years later, at the age of fourteen, he had no less than five hives standing neatly in a row against the fence in his father's small back yard, and already – apart from the normal task of producing honey – he was practising the delicate and complicated business of rearing his own queens, grafting larvae into artificial cell cups, and all the rest of it.

He never had to use smoke when there was work to do inside a hive, and he never wore gloves on his hands or a net over his head. Clearly there was some strange sympathy between this boy and the bees, and down in the village, in the shops and pubs, they began to speak about him with a certain kind of respect, and people started coming up to the house to buy his honey.

When he was eighteen, he had rented one acre of rough pasture alongside a cherry orchard down the valley about a mile from the village, and there he had set out to establish his own business. Now, eleven years later, he was still in the same spot, but he had six acres of ground instead of one, two hundred and forty well-stocked hives, and a small house that he'd built mainly with his own hands. He had married at the age of twenty and that, apart from the fact that it had taken them over nine years to get a child, had also been a success. In fact everything had gone pretty well for Albert until this strange little baby girl came along and started frightening them out of their wits by refusing to eat properly and losing weight every day.

He looked up from the magazine and began thinking about his daughter.

This evening, for instance, when she had opened her eyes at the beginning of the feed, he had gazed into them and seen something that frightened him to death – a kind of misty vacant stare, as though the eyes themselves were not connected to the brain at all but were just lying loose in their sockets like a couple of small grey marbles.

Did those doctors really know what they were talking about?

He reached for an ashtray and started slowly picking the ashes out from the bowl of his pipe with a matchstick.

One could always take her along to another hospital, somewhere in Oxford perhaps. He might suggest that to Mabel when he went upstairs.

He could still hear her moving around in the bedroom, but she must have taken off her shoes now and put on slippers because the noise was very faint.

He switched his attention back to the magazine and went on with his reading. He finished an article called 'Experiences in the Control of Nosema', then turned over the page and began reading the next one, 'The Latest on Royal Jelly'. He doubted very much whether there would be anything in this that he didn't know already:

'What is this wonderful substance called royal jelly?'

He reached for the tin of tobacco on the table beside him and began filling his pipe, still reading.

Royal jelly is a glandular secretion produced by the nurse bees to feed the larvae immediately they have hatched from the egg. The pharyngeal glands of bees produce this substance in much the same way as the mammary glands of vertebrates produce milk. The fact is of great biological interest because no other insects in the world are known to have evolved such a process.

All old stuff, he told himself, but for want of anything better to do, he continued to read.

Royal jelly is fed in concentrated form to all bee larvae for the first three days after hatching from the egg: but beyond that point, for all those who are destined to become drones or workers, this precious food is greatly diluted with honey and pollen. On the other hand, the larvae which are destined to become queens are fed throughout the whole of their larval period on a concentrated diet of pure royal jelly. Hence the name.

Above him, up in the bedroom, the noise of the footsteps had stopped altogether. The house was quiet. He struck a match and put it to his pipe.

Royal jelly must be a substance of tremendous nourishing power, for on this diet alone, the honey-bee larva increases in weight fifteen hundred times in five days.

That was probably about right, he thought, although for some reason it had never occurred to him to consider larval growth in terms of weight before.

This is as if a seven-and-a-half-pound baby should increase in that time to five tons.

Albert Taylor stopped and read that sentence again.
He read it a third time.
*This is as if a seven-and-a-half-pound baby . . .*
'Mabel!' he cried, jumping up from his chair. 'Mabel! Come here!'

He went out into the hall and stood at the foot of the stairs calling for her to come down.

There was no answer.

He ran up the stairs and switched on the light on the landing. The bedroom door was closed. He crossed the landing and opened it and stood in the doorway looking into the dark room. 'Mabel,' he said. 'Come downstairs a moment, will you please? I've just had a bit of an idea. It's about the baby.'

The light from the landing behind him cast a faint glow over the bed and he could see her dimly now, lying on her stomach with her face buried in the pillow and her arms up over her head. She was crying again.

'Mabel,' he said, going over to her, touching her shoulder. 'Please come down a moment. This may be important.'

'Go away,' she said. 'Leave me alone.'

'Don't you want to hear about my idea?'

'Oh, Albert, I'm *tired*,' she sobbed. 'I'm so tired I don't know what I'm doing any more. I don't think I can go on. I don't think I can stand it.'

There was a pause. Albert Taylor turned away from her and walked slowly over to the cradle where the baby was lying, and peered in. It was too dark for him to see the child's face, but when he bent down close he could hear the sound of breathing, very faint and quick. 'What time is the next feed?' he asked.

'Two o'clock, I suppose.'

'And the one after that?'

'Six in the morning.'

'I'll do them both,' he said. 'You go to sleep.'

She didn't answer.

'You get properly into bed, Mabel, and go straight to sleep, you understand? And stop worrying. I'm taking over completely for the next twelve hours. You'll give yourself a nervous breakdown going on like this.'

'Yes,' she said. 'I know.'

'I'm taking the nipper and myself *and* the alarm clock into the spare room this very moment, so you just lie down and relax and forget all about us. Right?' Already he was pushing the cradle out through the door.

'Oh, Albert,' she sobbed.

'Don't you worry about a thing. Leave it to me.'

'Albert . . .'

'Yes?'

'I love you, Albert.'

'I love you too, Mabel. Now go to sleep.'

Albert Taylor didn't see his wife again until nearly eleven o'clock the next morning.

'Good *gracious* me!' she cried, rushing down the stairs in dressing-gown and slippers. 'Albert! Just look at the time! I must have slept twelve hours at least! Is everything all right? What happened?'

41

He was sitting quietly in his armchair, smoking a pipe and reading the morning paper. The baby was in a sort of carrier cot on the floor at his feet, sleeping.

'Hullo, dear,' he said, smiling.

She ran over to the cot and looked in. 'Did she take anything, Albert? How many times have you fed her? She was due for another one at ten o'clock, did you know that?'

Albert Taylor folded the newspaper neatly into a square and put it away on the side table. 'I fed her at two in the morning,' he said, 'and she took about half an ounce, no more. I fed her again at six and she did a bit better that time, two ounces . . .'

'*Two ounces!* Oh, Albert, that's marvellous!'

'And we just finished the last feed ten minutes ago. There's the bottle on the mantelpiece. Only one ounce left. She drank three. How's that?' He was grinning proudly, delighted with his achievement.

The woman quickly got down on her knees and peered at the baby.

'Don't she look better?' he asked eagerly. 'Don't she look fatter in the face?'

'It may sound silly,' the wife said, 'but I actually think she does. Oh, Albert, you're a marvel! How did you do it?'

'She's turning the corner,' he said. 'That's all it is. Just like the doctor prophesied, she's turning the corner.'

'I pray to God you're right, Albert.'

'Of course I'm right. From now on, you watch her go.'

The woman was gazing lovingly at the baby.

'You look a lot better yourself too, Mabel.'

'I feel wonderful. I'm sorry about last night.'

'Let's keep it this way,' he said. 'I'll do all the night feeds in future. You do the day ones.'

She looked up at him across the cot, frowning. 'No,' she said. 'Oh no, I wouldn't allow you to do that.'

'I don't want you to have a breakdown, Mabel.'

'I won't, not now I've had some sleep.'

'Much better we share it.'

'No, Albert. This is my job and I intend to do it. Last night won't happen again.'

There was a pause. Albert Taylor took the pipe out of his mouth and examined the grain on the bowl. 'All right,' he said. 'In that case I'll just relieve you of the donkey work, I'll do all the sterilizing and the mixing of the food and getting everything ready. That'll help you a bit, anyway.'

She looked at him carefully, wondering what could have come over him all of a sudden.

'You see, Mabel, I've been thinking . . .'

'Yes, dear.'

'I've been thinking that up until last night I've never even raised a finger to help you with this baby.'

'That isn't true.'

'Oh yes it is. So I've decided that from now on I'm going to do *my* share of the work. I'm going to be the feed-mixer and the bottle-sterilizer. Right?'

'It's very sweet of you, dear, but I really don't think it's necessary . . .'

'Come on!' he cried. 'Don't change the luck! I done it

the last three times and just *look* what happened! When's the next one? Two o'clock, isn't it?'

'Yes.'

'It's all mixed,' he said. 'Everything's all mixed and ready and all you've got to do when the time comes is to go out there to the larder and take it off the shelf and warm it up. That's *some* help, isn't it?'

The woman got up off her knees and went over to him and kissed him on the cheek. 'You're such a nice man,' she said. 'I love you more and more every day I know you.'

Later, in the middle of the afternoon, when Albert was outside in the sunshine working among the hives, he heard her calling to him from the house.

'Albert!' she shouted. 'Albert, come here!' She was running through the buttercups towards him.

He started forward to meet her, wondering what was wrong.

'Oh, Albert! Guess what!'

'What?'

'I've just finished giving her the two-o'clock feed and she's taken the whole lot!'

'No!'

'Every drop of it! Oh, Albert, I'm so happy! She's going to be all right! She's turned the corner just like you said!' She came up to him and threw her arms round his neck and hugged him, and he clapped her on the back and laughed and said what a marvellous little mother she was.

'Will you come in and watch the next one and see if she does it again, Albert?'

He told her he wouldn't miss it for anything, and she hugged him again, then turned and ran back to the house, skipping over the grass and singing all the way.

Naturally, there was a certain amount of suspense in the air as the time approached for the six-o'clock feed. By five thirty both parents were already seated in the living-room waiting for the moment to arrive. The bottle with the milk formula in it was standing in a saucepan of warm water on the mantelpiece. The baby was asleep in its carrier cot on the sofa.

At twenty minutes to six it woke up and started screaming its head off.

'There you are!' Mrs Taylor cried. 'She's asking for the bottle. Pick her up quick, Albert, and hand her to me here. Give me the bottle first.'

He gave her the bottle, then placed the baby on the woman's lap. Cautiously, she touched the baby's lips with the end of the nipple. The baby seized the nipple between its gums and began to suck ravenously with a rapid powerful action.

'Oh, Albert, isn't it wonderful?' she said, laughing.

'It's terrific, Mabel.'

In seven or eight minutes, the entire contents of the bottle had disappeared down the baby's throat.

'You clever girl,' Mrs Taylor said. 'Four ounces again.'

Albert Taylor was leaning forward in his chair, peering intently into the baby's face. 'You know what?' he said. 'She even seems as though she's put on a touch of weight already. What do you think?'

The mother looked down at the child.

'Don't she seem bigger and fatter to you, Mabel, than she was yesterday?'

'Maybe she does, Albert. I'm not sure. Although actually there couldn't be any *real* gain in such a short time as this. The important thing is that she's eating normally.'

'She's turned the corner,' Albert said. 'I don't think you need worry about her any more.'

'I certainly won't.'

'You want me to go up and fetch the cradle back into our own bedroom, Mabel?'

'Yes, please,' she said.

Albert went upstairs and moved the cradle. The woman followed with the baby, and after changing its nappy, she laid it gently down on its bed. Then she covered it with sheet and blanket.

'Doesn't she look lovely, Albert?' she whispered. 'Isn't that the most beautiful baby you've ever seen in your *entire* life?'

'Leave her be now, Mabel,' he said. 'Come on downstairs and cook us a bit of supper. We both deserve it.'

After they had finished eating, the parents settled themselves in armchairs in the living-room, Albert with his magazine and his pipe, Mrs Taylor with her knitting. But this was a very different scene from the one of the night before. Suddenly, all tensions had vanished. Mrs Taylor's handsome oval face was glowing with pleasure, her cheeks were pink, her eyes were sparkling bright, and her mouth was fixed in a little dreamy smile of pure content. Every now and again she would glance up from her knitting and gaze affectionately at her husband. Occasionally, she would stop the clicking of her needles altogether for a few seconds and sit quite still, looking at the ceiling, listening for a cry or a whimper from upstairs. But all was quiet.

'Albert,' she said after a while.

'Yes, dear?'

'What was it you were going to tell me last night when you came rushing up to the bedroom? You said you had an idea for the baby.'

Albert Taylor lowered the magazine on to his lap and gave her a long sly look.

'Did I?' he said.

'Yes.' She waited for him to go on, but he didn't.

'What's the big joke?' she asked. 'Why are you grinning like that?'

'It's a joke all right,' he said.

'Tell it to me, dear.'

'I'm not sure I ought to,' he said. 'You might call me a liar.'

She had seldom seen him looking so pleased with himself as he was now, and she smiled back at him, egging him on.

'I'd just like to see your face when you hear it, Mabel, that's all.'

'Albert, what *is* all this?'

He paused, refusing to be hurried.

'You do think the baby's better, don't you?' he asked.

'Of course I do.'

'You agree with me that all of a sudden she's feeding marvellously and looking one hundred per cent different?'

'I do, Albert, yes.'

'That's good,' he said, the grin widening. 'You see, it's me that did it.'

'Did what?'

'I cured the baby.'

'Yes, dear, I'm sure you did.' Mrs Taylor went right on with her knitting.

'You don't believe me, do you?'

'Of course I believe you, Albert. I give you all the credit, every bit of it.'

'Then how did I do it?'

'Well,' she said, pausing a moment to think. 'I suppose it's simply that you're a brilliant feed-mixer. Ever since you started mixing the feeds she's got better and better.'

'You mean there's some sort of an art in mixing the feeds?'

'Apparently there is.' She was knitting away and smiling quietly to herself, thinking how funny men were.

'I'll tell you a secret,' he said. 'You're absolutely right. Although, mind you, it isn't so much *how* you mix it that counts. It's what you put in. You realize that, don't you, Mabel?'

Mrs Taylor stopped knitting and looked up sharply at her husband. 'Albert,' she said, 'don't tell me you've been putting things into that child's milk?'

He sat there grinning.

'Well, have you or haven't you?'

'It's possible,' he said.

'I don't believe it.'

He had a strange fierce way of grinning that showed his teeth.

'Albert,' she said. 'Stop playing with me like this.'

48

'Yes, dear, all right.'

'You haven't *really* put anything into her milk, have you? Answer me properly, Albert. This could be serious with such a tiny baby.'

'The answer is yes, Mabel.'

'*Albert Taylor!* How could you?'

'Now don't get excited,' he said. 'I'll tell you all about it if you really want me to, but for heaven's sake keep your hair on.'

'It was beer!' she cried. 'I just know it was beer!'

'Don't be so daft, Mabel, please.'

'Then what was it?'

Albert laid his pipe down carefully on the table beside him and leaned back in his chair. 'Tell me,' he said, 'did you ever by any chance happen to hear me mentioning something called royal jelly?'

'I did not.'

'It's magic,' he said. 'Pure magic. And last night I suddenly got the idea that if I was to put some of this into the baby's milk . . .'

'How *dare* you!'

'Now, Mabel, you don't even know what it is yet.'

'I don't care what it is,' she said. 'You can't go putting foreign bodies like that into a tiny baby's milk. You must be mad.'

'It's perfectly harmless, Mabel, otherwise I wouldn't have done it. It comes from bees.'

'I might have guessed that.'

'And it's so precious that practically no one can afford to take it. When they do, it's only one little drop at a time.'

'And how much did you give to our baby, might I ask?'

'Ah,' he said, 'that's the whole point. That's where the difference lies. I reckon that our baby, just in the last four feeds, has already swallowed about fifty times as much royal jelly as anyone else in the world has ever swallowed before. How about that?'

'Albert, stop pulling my leg.'

'I swear it,' he said proudly.

She sat there staring at him, her brow wrinkled, her mouth slightly open.

'You know what this stuff actually costs, Mabel, if you want to buy it? There's a place in America advertising it for sale this very moment for something like five hundred dollars a pound jar! *Five hundred dollars!* That's more than gold, you know!'

She hadn't the faintest idea what he was talking about.

'I'll prove it,' he said, and he jumped up and went across to the large bookcase where he kept all his literature about bees. On the top shelf, the back numbers of the *American Bee Journal* were neatly stacked alongside those of the *British Bee Journal*, *Beecraft*, and other magazines. He took down the last issue of the *American Bee Journal* and turned to a page of small classified advertisements at the back.

'Here you are,' he said. 'Exactly as I told you. "We sell royal jelly – $480 per lb jar wholesale."'

He handed her the magazine so she could read it herself.

'Now do you believe me? This is an actual shop in New York, Mabel. It says so.'

'It doesn't say you can go stirring it into the milk of a

practically newborn baby,' she said. 'I don't know what's come over you, Albert, I really don't.'

'It's curing her, isn't it?'

'I'm not so sure about that, now.'

'Don't be so damn silly, Mabel. You know it is.'

'Then why haven't other people done it with *their* babies?'

'I keep telling you,' he said. 'It's too expensive. Practically nobody in the world can afford to buy royal jelly just for *eating* except maybe one or two multimillionaires. The people who buy it are the big companies that make women's face creams and things like that. They're using it as a stunt. They mix a tiny pinch of it into a big jar of face cream and it's selling like hot cakes for absolutely enormous prices. They claim it takes out the wrinkles.'

'And does it?'

'Now how on earth would I know that, Mabel? Anyway,' he said, returning to his chair, 'that's not the point. The point is this. It's done so much good to our little baby just in the last few hours that I think we ought to go right on giving it to her. Now don't interrupt, Mabel. Let me finish. I've got two hundred and forty hives out there and if I turn over maybe a hundred of them to making royal jelly, we ought to be able to supply her with all she wants.'

'Albert Taylor,' the woman said, stretching her eyes wide and staring at him. 'Have you gone out of your mind?'

'Just hear me through, will you please?'

'I forbid it,' she said, 'absolutely. You're not to give my baby another drop of that horrid jelly, you understand?'

'Now, Mabel . . .'

'And quite apart from that, we had a shocking honey crop last year, and if you go fooling around with those hives now, there's no telling what might not happen.'

'There's nothing wrong with my hives, Mabel.'

'You know very well we had only half the normal crop last year.'

'Do me a favour, will you?' he said. 'Let me explain some of the marvellous things this stuff does.'

'You haven't even told what it is yet.'

'All right, Mabel. I'll do that too. Will you listen? Will you give me a chance to explain it?'

She sighed and picked up her knitting once more. 'I suppose you might as well get it off your chest, Albert. Go on and tell me.'

He paused, a bit uncertain now how to begin. It wasn't going to be easy to explain something like this to a person with no detailed knowledge of apiculture at all.

'You know, don't you,' he said, 'that each colony has only one queen?'

'Yes.'

'And that this queen lays all the eggs?'

'Yes, dear. That much I know.'

'All right. Now the queen can actually lay two different kinds of eggs. You didn't know that, but she can. It's what we call one of the miracles of the hive. She can lay eggs that produce drones, and she can lay eggs that produce workers. Now if that isn't a miracle, Mabel, I don't know what is.'

'Yes, Albert, all right.'

'The drones are the males. We don't have to worry about them. The workers are all females. So is the queen, of course. But the workers are unsexed females, if you see what I mean. Their organs are completely undeveloped, whereas the queen is tremendously sexy. She can actually lay her own weight in eggs in a single day.'

He hesitated, marshalling his thoughts.

'Now what happens is this. The queen crawls around on the comb and lays her eggs in what we call cells. You know all those hundreds of little holes you see in a honeycomb? Well, a brood comb is just about the same except the cells don't have honey in them, they have eggs. She lays one egg to each cell, and in three days each of these eggs hatches out into a tiny grub. We call it a larva.

'Now, as soon as this larva appears, the nurse bees – they're young workers – all crowd round and start feeding it like mad. And you know what they feed it on?'

'Royal jelly,' Mabel answered patiently.

'Right!' he cried. 'That's exactly what they do feed it on. They get this stuff out of a gland in their heads and they start pumping it into the cell to feed the larva. And what happens then?'

He paused dramatically, blinking at her with his small watery-grey eyes. Then he turned slowly in his chair and reached for the magazine that he had been reading the night before.

'You want to know what happens then?' he asked, wetting his lips.

'I can hardly wait.'

' "Royal jelly," ' he read aloud, ' "must be a substance of

tremendous nourishing power, for on this diet alone, the honey-bee larva increases in weight *fifteen hundred times* in five days!"'

'How much?'

'*Fifteen hundred times*, Mabel. And you know what that means if you put it in terms of a human being? It means,' he said, lowering his voice, leaning forward, fixing her with those small pale eyes, 'it means that in five days a baby weighing seven and a half pounds to start off with would increase in weight to *five tons*!'

For the second time, Mrs Taylor stopped knitting.

'Now you mustn't take that too literally, Mabel.'

'Who says I mustn't?'

'It's just a scientific way of putting it, that's all.'

'Very well, Albert. Go on.'

'But that's only half the story,' he said. 'There's more to come. The really amazing thing about royal jelly, I haven't told you yet. I'm going to show you now how it can transform a plain dull-looking little worker bee with practically no sex organs at all into a great big beautiful fertile queen.'

'Are you saying our baby is dull-looking and plain?' she asked sharply.

'Now don't go putting words into my mouth, Mabel, please. Just listen to this. Did you know that the queen bee and the worker bee, although they are completely different when they grow up, are both hatched out of exactly the same kind of egg?'

'I don't believe that,' she said.

'It's true as I'm sitting here, Mabel, honest it is. Any

time the bees want a queen to hatch out of the egg instead of a worker, they can do it.'

'How?'

'Ah,' he said, shaking a thick forefinger in her direction. 'That's just what I'm coming to. That's the secret of the whole thing. Now – what do *you* think it is, Mabel, that makes this miracle happen?'

'Royal jelly,' she answered. 'You already told me.'

'Royal jelly it is!' he cried, clapping his hands and bouncing up on his seat. His big round face was glowing with excitement now, and two vivid patches of scarlet had appeared high up on each cheek.

'Here's how it works. I'll put it very simply for you. The bees want a new queen. So they build an extra-large cell, a queen cell we call it, and they get the old queen to lay one of her eggs in there. The other one thousand nine hundred and ninety-nine eggs she lays in ordinary worker cells. Now. As soon as these eggs hatch out into larvae, the nurse bees rally round and start pumping in the royal jelly. All of them get it, workers as well as queen. But here's the vital thing, Mabel, so listen carefully. Here's where the difference comes. The worker larvae only receive this special marvellous food for the *first three days* of their larval life. After that they have a complete change of diet. What really happens is they get weaned, except that it's not like an ordinary weaning because it's so sudden. After the third day they're put straight away on to more or less routine bees' food – a mixture of honey and pollen – and then about two weeks later they emerge from the cells as workers.

'But not so the larva in the queen cell! This one gets royal jelly *all the way through its larval life*. The nurse bees simply pour it into the cell, so much so in fact that the little larva is literally floating in it. And that's what makes it into a queen!'

'You can't prove it,' she said.

'Don't talk so damn silly, Mabel, please. Thousands of people have proved it time and time again, famous scientists in every country in the world. All you have to do is take a larva out of a worker cell and put it in a queen cell – that's what we call grafting – and just so long as the nurse bees keep it well supplied with royal jelly, then presto! – it'll grow up into a queen! And what makes it more marvellous still is the absolutely enormous difference between a queen and a worker when they grow up. The abdomen is a different shape. The sting is different. The legs are different. The . . .'

'In what way are the legs different?' she asked, testing him.

'The legs? Well, the workers have little pollen baskets on their legs for carrying the pollen. The queen has none. Now here's another thing. The queen has fully developed sex organs. The workers don't. And most amazing of all, Mabel, the queen lives for an average of four to six years. The worker hardly lives that many months. And all this difference simply because one of them got royal jelly and the other didn't!'

'It's pretty hard to believe,' she said, 'that a food can do all that.'

'Of course it's hard to believe. It's another of the miracles of the hive. In fact it's the biggest ruddy miracle of them all. It's such a hell of a big miracle that it's baffled the greatest men of science for hundreds of years. Wait a moment. Stay there. Don't move.'

Again he jumped up and went over to the bookcase and started rummaging among the books and magazines.

'I'm going to find you a few of the reports. Here we are. Here's one of them. Listen to this.' He started reading aloud from a copy of the *American Bee Journal*:

'"Living in Toronto at the head of a fine research laboratory given to him by the people of Canada in recognition of his truly great contribution to humanity in the discovery of insulin, Dr Frederick A. Banting became curious about royal jelly. He requested his staff to do a basic fractional analysis . . ."'

He paused.

'Well, there's no need to read it all, but here's what happened. Dr Banting and his people took some royal jelly from queen cells that contained two-day-old larvae, and then they started analysing it. And what d'you think they found?

'They found,' he said, 'that royal jelly contained phenols, sterols, glycerils, dextrose, *and* – now here it comes – and eighty to eighty-five per cent *unidentified* acids!'

He stood beside the bookcase with the magazine in his hand, smiling a funny little furtive smile of triumph, and his wife watched him, bewildered.

He was not a tall man; he had a thick plump pulpy-looking body that was built close to the ground on abbreviated legs. The legs were slightly bowed. The head was huge and round, covered with bristly short-cut hair, and the greater part of the face – now that he had given up shaving altogether – was hidden by a brownish yellow fuzz about an inch long. In one way and another, he was rather grotesque to look at, there was no denying that.

'Eighty to eighty-five per cent,' he said, 'unidentified acids. Isn't that fantastic?' He turned back to the bookshelf and began hunting through the other magazines.

'What does it mean, unidentified acids?'

'That's the whole point! No one knows! Not even Banting could find out. You've heard of Banting?'

'No.'

'He just happens to be about the most famous living doctor in the world today, that's all.'

Looking at him now as he buzzed around in front of the bookcase with his bristly head and his hairy face and his plump pulpy body, she couldn't help thinking that somehow, in some curious way, there was a touch of the bee about this man. She had often seen women grow to look like the horses that they rode, and she had noticed that people who bred birds or bull terriers or pomeranians frequently resembled in some small but startling manner the creature of their choice. But up until now it had never occurred to her that her husband might look like a bee. It shocked her a bit.

'And did Banting ever try to eat it,' she asked, 'this royal jelly?'

'Of course he didn't eat it, Mabel. He didn't have enough for that. It's too precious.'

'You know something?' she said, staring at him but

smiling a little all the same. 'You're getting to look just a teeny bit like a bee yourself, did you know that?'

He turned and looked at her.

'I suppose it's the beard mostly,' she said. 'I do wish you'd stop wearing it. Even the colour is sort of bee-ish, don't you think?'

'What the hell are you talking about, Mabel?'

'Albert,' she said. 'Your language.'

'Do you want to hear any more of this or don't you?'

'Yes, dear, I'm sorry. I was only joking. Do go on.'

He turned away again and pulled another magazine out of the bookcase and began leafing through the pages. 'Now just listen to this, Mabel. "In 1939, Heyl experimented with twenty-one-day-old rats, injecting them with royal jelly in varying amounts. As a result, he found a precocious follicular development of the ovaries directly in proportion to the quantity of royal jelly injected."'

'There!' she cried. 'I knew it!'

'Knew what?'

'I knew something terrible would happen.'

'Nonsense. There's nothing wrong with that. Now here's another, Mabel. "Still and Burdett found that a male rat which hitherto had been unable to breed, upon receiving a minute daily dose of royal jelly, became a father many times over."'

'Albert,' she cried, 'this stuff is *much* too strong to give to a baby! I don't like it at all.'

'Nonsense, Mabel.'

'Then why do they only try it out on rats, tell me that?

Why don't some of these famous scientists take it themselves? They're too clever, that's why. Do you think Dr Banting is going to risk finishing up with precious ovaries? Not him.'

'But they *have* given it to people, Mabel. Here's a whole article about it. Listen.' He turned the page and again began reading from the magazine. '"In Mexico, in 1953, a group of enlightened physicians began prescribing minute doses of royal jelly for such things as cerebral neuritis, arthritis, diabetes, autointoxication from tobacco, impotence in men, asthma, croup and gout . . . There are stacks of signed testimonials . . . A celebrated stockbroker in Mexico City contracted a particularly stubborn case of psoriasis. He became physically unattractive. His clients began to forsake him. His business began to suffer. In desperation he turned to royal jelly – one drop with every meal – and presto! – he was cured in a fortnight. A waiter in the Café Jena, also in Mexico City, reported that his father, after taking minute doses of this wonder substance in capsule form, sired a healthy boy child at the age of ninety. A bullfight promoter in Acapulco, finding himself landed with a rather lethargic-looking bull, injected it with one gram of royal jelly (an excessive dose) just before it entered the arena. Thereupon, the beast became so swift and savage that it promptly dispatched two picadors, three horses and a matador, and finally . . . "'

'Listen!' Mrs Taylor said, interrupting him. 'I think the baby's crying.'

Albert glanced up from his reading. Sure enough, a lusty yelling noise was coming from the bedroom above.

'She must be hungry,' he said.

His wife looked at the clock. 'Good gracious me!' she cried, jumping up. 'It's past her time again already! You mix the feed, Albert, quickly, while I bring her down! But hurry! I don't want to keep her waiting.'

In half a minute, Mrs Taylor was back, carrying the screaming infant in her arms. She was flustered now, still quite unaccustomed to the ghastly non-stop racket that a healthy baby makes when it wants its food. 'Do be quick, Albert!' she called, settling herself in the armchair and arranging the child on her lap. 'Please hurry!'

Albert entered from the kitchen and handed her the bottle of warm milk. 'It's just right,' he said. 'You don't have to test it.'

She hitched the baby's head a little higher in the crook of her arm, then pushed the rubber teat straight into the wide-open yelling mouth. The baby grabbed the teat and began to suck. The yelling stopped. Mrs Taylor relaxed.

'Oh, Albert, isn't she lovely?'

'She's terrific, Mabel – thanks to royal jelly.'

'Now, dear, I don't want to hear another word about that nasty stuff. It frightens me to death.'

'You're making a big mistake,' he said.

'We'll see about that.'

The baby went on sucking the bottle.

'I do believe she's going to finish the whole lot again, Albert.'

'I'm sure she is,' he said.

And a few minutes later, the milk was all gone.

'Oh, what a good girl you are!' Mrs Taylor cried, as very

gently she started to withdraw the nipple. The baby sensed what she was doing and sucked harder, trying to hold on. The woman gave a quick little tug, and *plop*, out it came.

'Waa! Waa! Waa! Waa! Waa!' the baby yelled.

'Nasty old wind,' Mrs Taylor said, hoisting the child on to her shoulder and patting its back.

It belched twice in quick succession.

'There you are, my darling, you'll be all right now.'

For a few seconds, the yelling stopped. Then it started again.

'Keep belching her,' Albert said. 'She's drunk it too quick.'

His wife lifted the baby back on to her shoulder. She rubbed its spine. She changed it from one shoulder to the other. She lay it on its stomach on her lap. She sat it up on her knee. But it didn't belch again, and the yelling became louder and more insistent every minute.

'Good for the lungs,' Albert Taylor said, grinning. 'That's the way they exercise their lungs, Mabel, did you know that?'

'There, there, there,' the wife said, kissing it all over the face. 'There, there, there.'

They waited another five minutes, but not for one moment did the screaming stop.

'Change the nappy,' Albert said. 'It's got a wet nappy, that's all it is.' He fetched a clean one from the kitchen, and Mrs Taylor took the old one off and put the new one on.

This made no difference at all.

'Waa! Waa! Waa! Waa! Waa!' the baby yelled.

'You didn't stick the safety pin through the skin, did you, Mabel?'

'Of course I didn't,' she said, feeling under the nappy with her fingers to make sure.

The parents sat opposite one another in their armchairs, smiling nervously, watching the baby on the mother's lap, waiting for it to tire and stop screaming.

'You know what?' Albert Taylor said at last.

'What?'

'I'll bet she's still hungry. I'll bet all she wants is another swig at that bottle. How about me fetching her an extra lot?'

'I don't think we ought to do that, Albert.'

'It'll do her good,' he said, getting up from his chair. 'I'm going to warm her up a second helping.'

He went into the kitchen, and was away several minutes. When he returned he was holding a bottle brimful of milk.

'I made her a double,' he announced. 'Eight ounces. Just in case.'

'Albert! Are you mad! Don't you know it's just as bad to overfeed as it is to underfeed?'

'You don't have to give her the lot, Mabel. You can stop any time you like. Go on,' he said, standing over her. 'Give her a drink.'

Mrs Taylor began to tease the baby's lip with the end of the nipple. The tiny mouth closed like a trap over the rubber teat and suddenly there was silence in the room. The baby's whole body relaxed and a look of absolute bliss came over its face as it started to drink.

'There you are, Mabel! What did I tell you?'

The woman didn't answer.

'She's ravenous, that's what she is. Just look at her suck.'

Mrs Taylor was watching the level of the milk in the bottle. It was dropping fast, and before long three or four ounces out of the eight had disappeared.

'There,' she said. 'That'll do.'

'You can't pull it away now, Mabel.'

'Yes, dear. I must.'

'Go on, woman. Give her the rest and stop fussing.'

'But *Albert* . . .'

'She's famished, can't you see that? Go on, my beauty,' he said. 'You finish that bottle.'

'I don't like it, Albert,' the wife said, but she didn't pull the bottle away.

'She's making up for lost time, Mabel, that's all she's doing.'

Five minutes later the bottle was empty. Slowly, Mrs Taylor withdrew the nipple, and this time there was no protest from the baby, no sound at all. It lay peacefully on the mother's lap, the eyes glazed with contentment, the mouth half open, the lips smeared with milk.

'Twelve whole ounces, Mabel!' Albert Taylor said. 'Three times the normal amount! Isn't that amazing!'

The woman was staring down at the baby. And now the old anxious tight-lipped look of the frightened mother was slowly returning to her face.

'What's the matter with *you*?' Albert asked. 'You're not worried by that, are you? You can't expect her to get back to normal on a lousy four ounces, don't be ridiculous.'

'Come here, Albert,' she said.

'What?'

'I said come here.'

He went over and stood beside her.

'Take a good look and tell me if you see anything different.'

He peered closely at the baby. 'She seems bigger, Mabel, if that's what you mean. Bigger and fatter.'

'Hold her,' she ordered. 'Go on, pick her up.'

He reached out and lifted the baby up off the mother's lap. 'Good God!' he cried. 'She weighs a ton!'

'Exactly.'

'Now isn't that marvellous!' he cried, beaming. 'I'll bet she must almost be back to normal already!'

'It frightens me, Albert. It's too quick.'

'Nonsense, woman.'

'It's that disgusting jelly that's done it,' she said. 'I hate the stuff.'

'There's nothing disgusting about royal jelly,' he answered, indignant.

'Don't be a fool, Albert! You think it's *normal* for a child to start putting on weight at this speed?'

'You're never satisfied!' he cried. 'You're scared stiff when she's losing and now you're absolutely terrified because she's gaining! What's the matter with you, Mabel?'

The woman got up from her chair with the baby in her arms and started towards the door. 'All I can say is,' she said, 'it's lucky I'm here to see you don't give her any more of it, that's all I can say.' She went out, and Albert watched her through the open door as she crossed the hall to the foot of the stairs and started to ascend, and when she reached the third or fourth step she suddenly stopped and stood quite still for several seconds as though remembering something. Then she turned and came down again rather quickly and re-entered the room.

'Albert,' she said.

'Yes?'

'I assume there wasn't any royal jelly in this last feed we've just given her?'

'I don't see why you should assume that, Mabel.'

'Albert!'

'What's wrong?' he asked, soft and innocent.

'How *dare* you!' she cried.

Albert Taylor's great bearded face took on a pained and puzzled look. 'I think you ought to be very glad she's got another big dose of it inside her,' he said. 'Honest I do. And this *is* a big dose, Mabel, believe you me.'

The woman was standing just inside the doorway clasping the sleeping baby in her arms and staring at her husband with huge eyes. She stood very erect, her body absolutely stiff with fury, her face paler, more tight-lipped than ever.

'You mark my words,' Albert was saying, 'you're going to have a nipper there soon that'll win first prize in any baby show in the *entire* country. Hey, why don't you weigh her now and see what she is? You want me to get the scales, Mabel, so you can weigh her?'

The woman walked straight over to the large table in the centre of the room and laid the baby down and quickly started taking off its clothes. 'Yes!' she snapped. 'Get the scales!' Off came the little nightgown, then the undervest.

Then she unpinned the nappy and she drew it away and the baby lay naked on the table.

'But Mabel!' Albert cried. 'It's a miracle! She's fat as a puppy!'

Indeed, the amount of flesh the child had put on since the day before was astounding. The small sunken chest with the rib-bones showing all over it was now plump and round as a barrel, and the belly was bulging high in the air. Curiously, though, the arms and legs did not seem to have grown in proportion. Still short and skinny, they looked like little sticks protruding from a ball of fat.

'Look!' Albert said. 'She's even beginning to get a bit of fuzz on the tummy to keep her warm!' He put out a hand and was about to run the tips of his fingers over the powdering of silky yellowy-brown hairs that had suddenly appeared on the baby's stomach.

'*Don't you touch her!*' the woman cried. She turned and faced him, her eyes blazing, and she looked suddenly like some kind of a little fighting bird with her neck arched over towards him as though she were about to fly at his face and peck his eyes out.

'Now wait a minute,' he said, retreating.

'You must be mad!' she cried.

'Now wait just one minute, Mabel, will you please,

because if you're still thinking this stuff is dangerous . . .
That is what you're thinking, isn't it? All right, then. Listen
carefully. I shall now proceed to *prove* to you once and for
all, Mabel, that royal jelly is absolutely harmless to human
beings, even in enormous doses. For example – why do
you think we had only half the usual honey crop last
summer? Tell me that.'

His retreat, walking backwards, had taken him three or
four yards away from her, where he seemed to feel more
comfortable.

'The reason we had only half the usual crop last summer,' he said slowly, lowering his voice, 'was because I
turned one hundred of my hives over to the production
of royal jelly.'

'You *what?*'

'Ah,' he whispered. 'I thought that might surprise you a
bit. And I've been making it ever since right under your
very nose.' His small eyes were glinting at her, and a slow
sly smile was creeping round the corners of his mouth.

'You'll never guess the reason, either,' he said. 'I've
been afraid to mention it up to now because I thought it
might . . . well . . . sort of embarrass you.'

There was a slight pause. He had his hands clasped
high in front of him, level with his chest, and he was rubbing one palm against the other, making a soft scraping
noise.

'You remember that bit I read you out of the magazine? That bit about the rat? Let me see now, how does it
go? "Still and Burdett found that a male rat which hitherto

had been unable to breed ... "' He hesitated, the grin widening, showing his teeth.

'You get the message, Mabel?'

She stood quite still, facing him.

'The very first time I ever read that sentence, Mabel, I jumped straight out of my chair and I said to myself if it'll work with a lousy rat, I said, then there's no reason on earth why it shouldn't work with Albert Taylor.'

He paused again, craning his head forward and turning one ear slightly in his wife's direction, waiting for her to say something. But she didn't.

'And here's another thing,' he went on. 'It made me feel so absolutely marvellous, Mabel, and so sort of completely different to what I was before that I went right on taking it even after you'd announced the joyful tidings. *Buckets* of it I must have swallowed during the last twelve months.'

The big heavy haunted-looking eyes of the woman were moving intently over the man's face and neck. There was no skin showing at all on the neck, not even at the sides below the ears. The whole of it, to a point where it disappeared into the collar of the shirt, was covered all the way round with those shortish silky hairs, yellowly black.

'Mind you,' he said, turning away from her, gazing lovingly now at the baby, 'it's going to work far better on a tiny infant than on a fully developed man like me. You've only got to look at her to see that, don't you agree?'

The woman's eyes travelled slowly downwards and

settled on the baby. The baby was lying naked on the table, fat and white and comatose, like some gigantic grub that was approaching the end of its larval life and would soon emerge into the world complete with mandibles and wings.

'Why don't you cover her up, Mabel?' he said. 'We don't want our little queen to catch a cold.'

# Mrs Bixby and the Colonel's Coat

First published in *Nugget* (1959)

America is the land of opportunity for women. Already they own about eighty-five per cent of the wealth of the nation. Soon they will have it all. Divorce has become a lucrative process, simple to arrange and easy to forget; and ambitious females can repeat it as often as they please and parlay their winnings to astronomical figures. The husband's death also brings satisfactory rewards and some ladies prefer to rely upon this method. They know that the waiting period will not be unduly protracted, for overwork and hypertension are bound to get the poor devil before long, and he will die at his desk with a bottle of benzedrines in one hand and a packet of tranquillizers in the other.

Succeeding generations of youthful American males are not deterred in the slightest by this terrifying pattern of divorce and death. The higher the divorce rate climbs, the more eager they become. Young men marry like mice, almost before they have reached the age of puberty, and a large proportion of them have at least two ex-wives on the payroll by the time they are thirty-six years old. To support these ladies in the manner to which they are accustomed, the men must work like slaves, which is of course precisely what they are. But now at last, as they approach their premature middle age, a sense of disillusionment and fear begins to creep slowly into their hearts, and in the evenings they take to huddling together in little groups, in clubs and bars, drinking their whiskies and swallowing their pills, and trying to comfort one another with stories.

The basic theme of these stories never varies. There are always three main characters – the husband, the wife and the dirty dog. The husband is a decent clean-living man, working hard at his job. The wife is cunning, deceitful and lecherous, and she is invariably up to some sort of jiggery-pokery with the dirty dog. The husband is too good a man even to suspect her. Things look black for the husband. Will the poor man ever find out? Must he be a cuckold for the rest of his life? Yes, he must. But wait! Suddenly, by a brilliant manoeuvre, the husband completely turns the tables on his monstrous spouse. The woman is flabbergasted, stupefied, humiliated, defeated. The audience of men around the bar smiles quietly to itself and takes a little comfort from the fantasy.

There are many of these stories going around, these wonderful wishful-thinking dreamworld inventions of the unhappy male, but most of them are too fatuous to be worth repeating, and far too fruity to be put down on paper. There is one, however, that seems to be superior to the rest, particularly as it has the merit of being true. It is extremely popular with twice- or thrice-bitten males in search of solace, and if you are one of them, and if you haven't heard it before, you may enjoy the way it comes out. The story is called 'Mrs Bixby and the Colonel's Coat', and it goes something like this:

Dr and Mrs Bixby lived in a smallish apartment some-where in New York City. Dr Bixby was a dentist who made an average income. Mrs Bixby was a big vigorous woman with a wet mouth. Once a month, always on Friday afternoons, Mrs Bixby would board the train at Pennsylvania Station and travel to Baltimore to visit her old aunt. She would spend the night with the aunt and return to New York on the following day in time to cook supper for her husband. Dr Bixby accepted this arrange-ment good-naturedly. He knew that Aunt Maude lived in Baltimore, and that his wife was very fond of the old lady, and certainly it would be unreasonable to deny either of them the pleasure of a monthly meeting.

'Just so long as you don't ever expect me to accompany you,' Dr Bixby had said in the beginning.

'Of course not, darling,' Mrs Bixby had answered. 'After all, she is not *your* aunt. She's mine.'

So far so good.

At it turned out, however, the aunt was little more than a convenient alibi for Mrs Bixby. The dirty dog, in the shape of a gentleman known as the Colonel, was lurking slyly in the background, and our heroine spent the greater part of her Baltimore time in this scoundrel's company. The Colonel was exceedingly wealthy. He lived in a charm-ing house on the outskirts of the town. No wife or family encumbered him, only a few discreet and loyal servants, and in Mrs Bixby's absence he consoled himself by riding his horses and hunting the fox.

Year after year, this pleasant alliance between Mrs Bixby and the Colonel continued without a hitch. They met so seldom – twelve times a year is not much when you come to think of it – that there was little or no chance of their growing bored with one another. On the contrary, the long wait between meetings only made the heart grow fonder, and each separate occasion became an exciting reunion.

'Tally-ho!' the Colonel would cry each time he met her at the station in the big car. 'My dear, I'd almost forgotten how ravishing you looked. Let's go to earth.'

Eight years went by.

It was just before Christmas, and Mrs Bixby was standing on the station in Baltimore waiting for the train to take her back to New York. This particular visit which had just ended had been more than usually agreeable, and she was in a cheerful mood. But then the Colonel's company always did that to her these days. The man had a way of making her feel that she was altogether a rather remarkable woman, a person of subtle and exotic talents, fascinating beyond measure; and what a very different thing that was from the dentist husband at home who never succeeded in making her feel that she was anything but a sort of eternal patient, someone who dwelt in the waiting-room, silent among the magazines, seldom if ever nowadays to be called in to suffer the finicky precise ministrations of those clean pink hands.

'The Colonel asked me to give you this,' a voice beside her said. She turned and saw Wilkins, the Colonel's groom, a small wizened dwarf with grey skin, and he was pushing a large flattish cardboard box into her arms.

'Good gracious me!' she cried, all of a flutter. 'My

heavens, what an enormous box! What is it, Wilkins? Was there a message? Did he send me a message?'

'No message,' the groom said, and he walked away.

As soon as she was on the train, Mrs Bixby carried the box into the privacy of the Ladies' Room and locked the door. How exciting this was! A Christmas present from the Colonel. She started to undo the string. 'I'll bet it's a dress,' she said aloud. 'It might even be two dresses. Or it might be a whole lot of beautiful underclothes. I won't look. I'll just feel around and try to guess what it is. I'll try to guess the colour as well, and exactly what it looks like. Also how much it cost.'

She shut her eyes tight and slowly lifted off the lid. Then she put one hand down into the box. There was some tissue paper on top; she could feel it and hear it rustling. There was also an envelope or a card of some sort. She ignored this and began burrowing underneath the tissue paper, the fingers reaching out delicately, like tendrils.

'My God,' she cried suddenly. 'It can't be true!'

She opened her eyes wide and stared at the coat. Then she pounced on it and lifted it out of the box. Thick layers of fur made a lovely noise against the tissue paper as they unfolded, and when she held it up and saw it hanging to its full length, it was so beautiful it took her breath away.

Never had she seen mink like this before. It *was* mink, wasn't it? Yes, of course it was. But what a glorious colour! The fur was almost pure black. At first she thought it *was* black; but when she held it closer to the window she saw that there was a touch of blue in it as well, a deep rich blue, like cobalt. Quickly she looked at the label. It said simply, WILD LABRADOR MINK. There was nothing else, no sign of where it had been bought or anything. But that, she told herself, was probably the Colonel's doing. The wily old fox was making darn sure he didn't leave any tracks. Good for him. But what in the world could it have cost? She hardly dared to think. Four, five, six thousand dollars? Possibly more.

She just couldn't take her eyes off it. Nor, for that matter, could she wait to try it on. Quickly she slipped off her own plain red coat. She was panting a little now, she couldn't help it, and her eyes were stretched very wide. But oh God, the feel of that fur! And those huge wide sleeves with their thick turned-up cuffs! Who was it had once told her that they always used female skins for the arms and male skins for the rest of the coat? Someone had told her that. Joan Rutfield, probably; though how *Joan* would know anything about *mink* she couldn't imagine.

The great black coat seemed to slide on to her almost of its own accord, like a second skin. Oh boy! It was the queerest feeling! She glanced into the mirror. It was fantastic. Her whole personality had suddenly changed completely. She looked dazzling, radiant, rich, brilliant, voluptuous, all at the same time. And the sense of power that it gave her! In this coat she could walk into any place she wanted and people would come scurrying around her like rabbits. The whole thing was just too wonderful for words!

Mrs Bixby picked up the envelope that was still lying in the box. She opened it and pulled out the Colonel's letter:

*I once heard you saying you were fond of mink so I got you this.*
*I'm told it's a good one. Please accept it with my sincere good*
*wishes as a parting gift. For my own personal reasons I shall not*
*be able to see you any more. Good-bye and good luck.*

Well!

Imagine that!

Right out of the blue, just when she was feeling so happy.

No more Colonel.

What a dreadful shock.

She would miss him enormously.

Slowly, Mrs Bixby began stroking the lovely soft black fur of the coat. What you lose on the swings you get back on the roundabouts.

She smiled and folded the letter, meaning to tear it up and throw it out the window, but in folding it she noticed that there was something written on the other side:

*P.S. Just tell them that nice generous aunt of yours gave it to you*
*for Christmas.*

Mrs Bixby's mouth, at that moment stretched wide in a silky smile, snapped back like a piece of elastic.

'The man must be mad!' she cried. 'Aunt Maude doesn't have that sort of money. She couldn't possibly give me this.'

But if Aunt Maude didn't give it to her, then who did?

Oh God! In the excitement of finding the coat and trying it on, she had completely overlooked this vital aspect.

In a couple of hours she would be in New York. Ten minutes after that she would be home, and the husband would be there to greet her; and even a man like Cyril, dwelling as he did in a dark phlegmy world of root canals, bicuspids and caries, would start asking a few questions if his wife suddenly waltzed in from a week-end wearing a six-thousand-dollar mink coat.

You know what I think, she told herself. I think that goddam Colonel has done this on purpose just to torture me. He knew perfectly well Aunt Maude didn't have enough money to buy this. He knew I wouldn't be able to keep it.

But the thought of parting with it now was more than Mrs Bixby could bear.

'I've *got* to have this coat!' she said aloud. 'I've got to have this coat! I've got to have this coat!'

Very well, my dear. You shall have the coat. But don't panic. Sit still and keep calm and start thinking. You're a clever girl, aren't you? You've fooled him before. The man never has been able to see much further than the end of his own probe, you know that. So just sit absolutely still and *think*. There's lots of time.

Two and a half hours later, Mrs Bixby stepped off the train at Pennsylvania Station and walked quickly to the exit. She was wearing her old red coat again now and carrying the cardboard box in her arms. She signalled for a taxi.

'Driver,' she said, 'would you know of a pawnbroker that's still open around here?'

The man behind the wheel raised his brows and looked back at her, amused.

'Plenty along Sixth Avenue,' he answered.

'Stop at the first one you see, then, will you please?' She got in and was driven away.

Soon the taxi pulled up outside a shop that had three brass balls hanging over the entrance.

'Wait for me, please,' Mrs Bixby said to the driver, and she got out of the taxi and entered the shop.

There was an enormous cat crouching on the counter eating fishheads out of a white saucer. The animal looked up at Mrs Bixby with bright yellow eyes, then looked away again and went on eating. Mrs Bixby stood by the counter, as far away from the cat as possible, waiting for someone to come, staring at the watches, the shoe buckles, the enamel brooches, the old binoculars, the broken spectacles, the false teeth. Why did they always pawn their teeth, she wondered.

'Yes?' the proprietor said, emerging from a dark place in the back of the shop.

'Oh, good evening,' Mrs Bixby said. She began to untie the string round the box. The man went up to the cat and started stroking it along the top of its back, and the cat went on eating the fishheads.

'Isn't it silly of me?' Mrs Bixby said. 'I've gone and lost my pocketbook, and this being Saturday, the banks are all closed until Monday and I've simply got to have some money for the week-end. This is quite a valuable coat, but I'm not asking much. I only want to borrow enough on it to tide me over till Monday. Then I'll come back and redeem it.'

The man waited, and said nothing. But when she pulled

out the mink and allowed the beautiful thick fur to fall over the counter, his eyebrows went up and he drew his hand away from the cat and came over to look at it. He picked it up and held it out in front of him.

'If only I had a watch on me or a ring,' Mrs Bixby said, 'I'd give you that instead. But the fact is I don't have a thing with me other than this coat.' She spread out her fingers for him to see.

'It looks new,' the man said, fondling the soft fur.

'Oh yes, it is. But, as I said, I only want to borrow enough to tide me over till Monday. How about fifty dollars?'

'I'll loan you fifty dollars.'

'It's worth a hundred times more than that, but I know you'll take good care of it until I return.'

The man went over to a drawer and fetched a ticket and placed it on the counter. The ticket looked like one of those labels you tie on to the handle of your suitcase, the same shape and size exactly, and the same stiff brownish paper. But it was perforated across the middle so that you could tear it in two, and both halves were identical.

'Name?' he asked.

'Leave that out. And the address.'

She saw the man pause, and she saw the nib of the pen hovering over the dotted line, waiting.

'You don't *have* to put the name and address, do you?'

The man shrugged and shook his head and the pen-nib moved on down to the next line.

'It's just that I'd rather not,' Mrs Bixby said. 'It's purely personal.'

'You'd better not lose this ticket, then.'

'I won't lose it.'

'You realize that anyone who gets hold of it can come in and claim the article?'

'Yes, I know that.'

'Simply on the number.'

'Yes, I know.'

'What do you want me to put for a description?'

'No description either, thank you. It's not necessary. Just put the amount I'm borrowing.'

The pen-nib hesitated again, hovering over the dotted line beside the word ARTICLE.

'I think you ought to put a description. A description is always a help if you want to sell the ticket. You never know, you might want to sell it sometime.'

'I don't want to sell it.'

'You might have to. Lots of people do.'

'Look,' Mrs Bixby said. 'I'm not broke, if that's what you mean. I simply lost my purse. Don't you understand?'

'You have it your own way then,' the man said. 'It's your coat.'

At this point an unpleasant thought struck Mrs Bixby. 'Tell me something,' she said. 'If I don't have a description on my ticket, how can I be sure you'll give me back the coat and not something else when I return?'

'It goes in the books.'

'But all I've got is a number. So actually you could hand me any old thing you wanted, isn't that so?'

'Do you want a description or don't you?' the man asked.

'No,' she said. 'I trust you.'

The man wrote 'fifty dollars' opposite the word VALUE on both sections of the ticket, then he tore it in half along the perforations and slid the lower portion across the counter. He took a wallet from the inside pocket of his jacket and extracted five ten-dollar bills. 'The interest is three per cent a month,' he said.

'Yes, all right. And thank you. You'll take good care of it, won't you?'

The man nodded but said nothing.

'Shall I put it back in the box for you?'

'No,' the man said.

Mrs Bixby turned and went out of the shop on to the street where the taxi was waiting. Ten minutes later, she was home.

'Darling,' she said as she bent over and kissed her husband. 'Did you miss me?'

Cyril Bixby laid down the evening paper and glanced at the watch on his wrist. 'It's twelve and a half minutes past six,' he said. 'You're a bit late, aren't you?'

'I know. It's those dreadful trains. Aunt Maude sent you her love as usual. I'm dying for a drink, aren't you?'

The husband folded his newspaper into a neat rectangle and placed it on the arm of his chair. Then he stood up and crossed over to the sideboard. His wife remained in the centre of the room pulling off her gloves, watching him carefully, wondering how long she ought to wait. He had his back to her now, bending forward to measure the gin, putting his face right up close to the measurer and peering into it as though it were a patient's mouth.

It was funny how small he always looked after the Colonel. The Colonel was huge and bristly, and when you were near to him he smelled faintly of horseradish. This one was small and neat and bony and he didn't really smell of anything at all, except peppermint drops, which he sucked to keep his breath nice for the patients.

'See what I've bought for measuring the vermouth,' he said, holding up a calibrated glass beaker. 'I can get it to the nearest milligram with this.'

'Darling, how clever.'

I really must try to make him change the way he dresses, she told herself. His suits are just too ridiculous for words. There had been a time when she thought they were wonderful, those Edwardian jackets with high lapels and six buttons down the front, but now they merely seemed absurd. So did the narrow stovepipe trousers. You had to have a special sort of face to wear things like that, and Cyril just didn't have it. His was a long bony countenance with a narrow nose and a slightly prognathous jaw, and when you saw it coming up out of the top of one of those tightly fitting old-fashioned suits it looked like a caricature of Sam Weller. He probably thought it looked like Beau Brummell. It was a fact that in the office he invariably greeted female patients with his white coat unbuttoned so that they would catch a glimpse of the trappings underneath; and in some obscure way this was obviously meant to convey the impression that he was a bit of a dog. But Mrs Bixby knew better. The plumage was a bluff. It meant nothing. It reminded her of an ageing peacock strutting on the lawn with only half its feathers left. Or one of those fatuous self-fertilizing flowers – like the dandelion. A dandelion never has to get fertilized for the setting of its seed, and all those brilliant yellow petals are just a waste of time, a boast, a masquerade. What's that word the biologists use? Subsexual. A dandelion is subsexual. So, for that matter, are the summer broods of water fleas. It sounds a bit like Lewis Carroll, she thought – water fleas and dandelions and dentists.

'Thank you, darling,' she said, taking the martini and seating herself on the sofa with her handbag on her lap. 'And what did *you* do last night?'

'I stayed on in the office and cast a few inlays. I also got my accounts up to date.'

'Now really, Cyril, I think it's high time you let other people do your donkey work for you. You're much too important for that sort of thing. Why don't you give the inlays to the mechanic?'

'I prefer to do them myself. I'm extremely proud of my inlays.'

'I know you are, darling, and I think they're absolutely wonderful. They're the best inlays in the whole world. But I don't want you to burn yourself out. And why doesn't that Pulteney woman do the accounts? That's part of her job, isn't it?'

'She does do them. But I have to price everything up first. She doesn't know who's rich and who isn't.'

'This martini is perfect,' Mrs Bixby said, setting down her glass on the side table. 'Quite perfect.' She opened her bag and took out a handkerchief as if to blow her nose.

'Oh look!' she cried, seeing the ticket. 'I forgot to show you this! I found it just now on the seat of my taxi. It's got a number on it, and I thought it might be a lottery ticket or something, so I kept it.'

She handed the small piece of stiff brown paper to her husband, who took it in his fingers and began examining it minutely from all angles, as though it were a suspect tooth.

'You know what this is?' he said slowly.

'No dear, I don't.'

'It's a pawn ticket.'

'A what?'

'A ticket from a pawnbroker. Here's the name and address of the shop – somewhere on Sixth Avenue.'

'Oh dear, I *am* disappointed. I was hoping it might be a ticket for the Irish Sweep.'

'There's no reason to be disappointed,' Cyril Bixby said. 'As a matter of fact this could be rather amusing.'

'Why could it be amusing, darling?'

He began explaining to her exactly how a pawn ticket worked, with particular reference to the fact that anyone possessing the ticket was entitled to claim the article. She listened patiently until he had finished his lecture.

'You think it's worth claiming?' she asked.

'I think it's worth finding out what it is. You see this figure of fifty dollars that's written here? You know what that means?'

'No, dear, what does it mean?'

'It means that the item in question is almost certain to be something quite valuable.'

'You mean it'll be worth fifty dollars?'

'More like five hundred.'

'Five hundred!'

'Don't you understand?' he said. 'A pawnbroker never gives you more than about a tenth of the real value.'

'Good gracious! I never knew that.'

'There's a lot of things you don't know, my dear. Now you listen to me. Seeing that there's no name and address of the owner . . .'

'But surely there's something to say who it belongs to?'

'Not a thing. People often do that. They don't want anyone to know they've been to a pawnbroker. They're ashamed of it.'

'Then you think we can keep it?'

'Of course we can keep it. This is now *our* ticket.'

'You mean *my* ticket,' Mrs Bixby said firmly. 'I found it.'

'My dear girl, what *does* it matter? The important thing is that we are now in a position to go and redeem it any time we like for only fifty dollars. How about that?'

'Oh, what fun!' she cried. 'I think it's terribly exciting, especially when we don't even know what it is. It could be *anything*, isn't that right, Cyril? Absolutely anything!'

'It could indeed, although it's most likely to be either a ring or a watch.'

'But wouldn't it be marvellous if it was a *real* treasure? I mean something *really* old, like a wonderful old vase or a Roman statue.'

'There's no knowing what it might be, my dear. We shall just have to wait and see.'

'I think it's absolutely fascinating! Give me the ticket

and I'll rush over first thing Monday morning and find out!'

'I think I'd better do that.'

'Oh no!' she cried. 'Let *me* do it!'

'I think not. I'll pick it up on my way to work.'

'But it's *my* ticket! *Please* let me do it, Cyril! Why should *you* have all the fun?'

'You don't know these pawnbrokers, my dear. You're liable to get cheated.'

'I wouldn't get cheated, honestly I wouldn't. Give it to me, please.'

'Also you have to have fifty dollars,' he said, smiling. 'You have to pay out fifty dollars in cash before they'll give it to you.'

'I've got that,' she said. 'I think.'

'I'd rather you didn't handle it, if you don't mind.'

'But Cyril, *I found* it. It's mine. Whatever it is, it's mine, isn't that right?'

'Of course it's yours, my dear. There's no need to get so worked up about it.'

'I'm not. I'm just excited, that's all.'

'I suppose it hasn't occurred to you that this might be something entirely masculine – a pocket-watch, for example, or a set of shirt-studs. It isn't only women that go to pawnbrokers, you know.'

'In that case I'll give it to you for Christmas,' Mrs Bixby said magnanimously. 'I'll be delighted. But if it's a woman's thing, I want it myself. Is that agreed?'

'That sounds very fair. Why don't you come with me when I collect it?'

Mrs Bixby was about to say yes to this, but caught herself just in time. She had no wish to be greeted like an old customer by the pawnbroker in her husband's presence.

'No,' she said slowly. 'I don't think I will. You see, it'll be even more thrilling if I stay behind and wait. Oh, I do hope it isn't going to be something that neither of us wants.'

'You've got a point there,' he said. 'If I don't think it's worth fifty dollars, I won't even take it.'

'But you said it would be worth five hundred.'

'I'm quite sure it will. Don't worry.'

'Oh, Cyril, I can hardly wait! Isn't it exciting?'

'It's amusing,' he said, slipping the ticket into his waistcoat pocket. 'There's no doubt about that.'

Monday morning came at last, and after breakfast Mrs Bixby followed her husband to the door and helped him on with his coat.

'Don't work too hard, darling,' she said.

'No, all right.'

'Home at six?'

'I hope so.'

'Are you going to have time to go to that pawnbroker?' she asked.

'My God, I forgot all about it. I'll take a cab and go there now. It's on my way.'

'You haven't lost the ticket, have you?'

'I hope not,' he said, feeling in his waistcoat pocket. 'No, here it is.'

'And you have enough money?'

'Just about.'

'Darling,' she said, standing close to him and straightening his tie, which was perfectly straight. 'If it happens to be something nice, something you think I might like, will you telephone me as soon as you get to the office?'

'If you want me to, yes.'

'You know, I'm sort of hoping it'll be something for you, Cyril. I'd much rather it was for you than for me.'

'That's very generous of you, my dear. Now I must run.'

About an hour later, when the telephone rang, Mrs Bixby was across the room so fast she had the receiver off the hook before the first ring had finished.

'I got it!' he said.

'You did! Oh, Cyril, what was it? Was it something good?'

'Good!' he cried. 'It's fantastic! You wait till you get your eyes on this! You'll swoon!'

'Darling, what is it? Tell me quick!'

'You're a lucky girl, that's what you are.'

'It's for me, then?'

'Of course it's for you. Though how in the world it ever got to be pawned for only fifty dollars I'll be damned if I know. Someone's crazy.'

'Cyril! Stop keeping me in suspense! I can't bear it!'

'You'll go mad when you see it.'

'What is it?'

'Try to guess.'

Mrs Bixby paused. Be careful, she told herself. Be very careful now.

'A necklace,' she said.

'Wrong.'

'A diamond ring.'

'You're not even warm. I'll give you a hint. It's something you can wear.'

'Something I can wear? You mean like a hat?'

'No, it's not a hat,' he said, laughing.

'For goodness' sake, Cyril! Why don't you tell me?'

'Because I want it to be a surprise. I'll bring it home with me this evening.'

'You'll do nothing of the sort!' she cried. 'I'm coming right down there to get it now!'

'I'd rather you didn't do that.'

'Don't be so silly, darling. Why shouldn't I come?'

'Because I'm too busy. You'll disorganize my whole morning schedule. I'm half an hour behind already.'

'Then I'll come in the lunch hour. All right?'

'I'm not having a lunch hour. Oh well, come at one thirty then, while I'm having a sandwich. Good-bye.'

At half past one precisely, Mrs Bixby arrived at Dr Bixby's place of business and rang the bell. Her husband, in his white dentist's coat, opened the door himself.

'Oh, Cyril, I'm so excited!'

'So you should be. You're a lucky girl, did you know that?' He led her down the passage and into the surgery.

'Go and have your lunch, Miss Pulteney,' he said to the assistant, who was busy putting instruments into the sterilizer. 'You can finish that when you come back.' He waited until the girl had gone, then he walked over to a closet that he used for hanging up his clothes and stood in front of it, pointing with his finger. 'It's in there,' he said. 'Now – shut your eyes.'

Mrs Bixby did as she was told. Then she took a deep breath and held it, and in the silence that followed she could hear him opening the cupboard door and there was a soft swishing sound as he pulled out a garment from among the other things hanging there.

'All right! You can look!'

'I don't dare to,' she said, laughing.

'Go on. Take a peek.'

Coyly, beginning to giggle, she raised one eyelid a fraction of an inch, just enough to give her a dark blurry view of the man standing there in his white overalls holding something up in the air.

'Mink!' he cried. 'Real mink!'

At the sound of the magic word she opened her eyes quick, and at the same time she actually started forward in order to clasp the coat in her arms.

But there was no coat. There was only a ridiculous little fur neckpiece dangling from her husband's hand.

'Feast your eyes on that!' he said, waving it in front of her face.

Mrs Bixby put a hand up to her mouth and started backing away. I'm going to scream, she told herself. I just know it. I'm going to scream.

'What's the matter, my dear? Don't you like it?' He stopped waving the fur and stood staring at her, waiting for her to say something.

'Why yes,' she stammered. 'I . . . I . . . think it's . . . it's lovely . . . really lovely.'

'Quite took your breath away for a moment there, didn't it?'

'Yes, it did.'

'Magnificent quality,' he said. 'Fine colour, too. You know something, my dear? I reckon a piece like this would cost you two or three hundred dollars at least if you had to buy it in a shop.'

'I don't doubt it.'

There were two skins, two narrow mangy-looking skins with their heads still on them and glass beads in their eye sockets and little paws hanging down. One of them had the rear end of the other in its mouth, biting it.

'Here,' he said. 'Try it on.' He leaned forward and draped the thing round her neck, then stepped back to admire. 'It's perfect. It really suits you. It isn't everyone who has mink, my dear.'

'No, it isn't.'

'Better leave it behind when you go shopping or they'll all think we're millionaires and start charging us double.'

'I'll try to remember that, Cyril.'

'I'm afraid you mustn't expect anything else for Christmas. Fifty dollars was rather more than I was going to spend anyway.'

He turned away and went over to the basin and began washing his hands. 'Run along now, my dear, and buy yourself a nice lunch. I'd take you out myself but I've got old man Gorman in the waiting-room with a broken clasp on his denture.'

Mrs Bixby moved towards the door.

I'm going to kill that pawnbroker, she told herself. I'm going right back there to the shop this very minute and I'm going to throw this filthy neckpiece right in his face and if he refuses to give me back my coat I'm going to kill him.

'Did I tell you I was going to be late home tonight?' Cyril Bixby said, still washing his hands.

'No.'

'It'll probably be at least eight thirty the way things look at the moment. It may even be nine.'

'Yes, all right. Good-bye.' Mrs Bixby went out, slamming the door behind her.

At that precise moment, Miss Pulteney, the secretary-assistant, came sailing past her down the corridor on her way to lunch.

'Isn't it a gorgeous day?' Miss Pulteney said as she went by, flashing a smile. There was a lilt in her walk, a little whiff of perfume attending her, and she looked like a queen, just exactly like a queen in the beautiful black mink coat that the Colonel had given to Mrs Bixby.

# The Swan

First published in *The Wonderful Story of
Henry Sugar* (1977)

Ernie had been given a .22 rifle for his birthday. His father,
who was already slouching on the sofa watching the telly
at nine thirty on this Saturday morning, said, 'Let's see
what you can pot, boy. Make yourself useful. Bring us
back a rabbit for supper.'

'There's rabbits in that big field the other side of the
lake,' Ernie said. 'I seen 'em.'

'Then go out and nab one,' the father said, picking
breakfast from between his front teeth with a split matchstick. 'Go out and nab us a rabbit.'

'I'll get yer two,' Ernie said.

'And on the way back,' the father said, 'get me a quart
bottle of brown ale.'

'Gimme the money, then,' Ernie said.

The father, without taking his eyes from the TV screen,
fished in his pocket for a pound note. 'And don't try
pinchin' the change like you did last time,' he said. 'You'll
get a thick ear if you do, birthday or no birthday.'

'Don't worry,' Ernie said.

'And if you want to practise and get your eye in with
that gun,' the father said, 'birds is best. See 'ow many
spadgers you can knock down, right?'

94

'Right,' Ernie said. 'There's spadgers all the way up the lane in the 'edges. Spadgers is easy.'

'If you think spadgers is easy,' the father said, 'go get yourself a jenny wren. Jenny wrens is 'alf the size of spadgers and they never sit still for one second. Get yourself a jenny wren before you start shootin' yer mouth off about 'ow clever you is.'

'Now, Albert,' his wife said, looking up from the sink. 'That's not nice, shootin' little birds in the nestin' season. I don't mind rabbits, but little birds in the nestin' season is another thing altogether.'

'Shut your mouth,' the father said. 'Nobody's askin' your opinion. And listen to me, boy,' he said to Ernie. 'Don't go waving that thing about in the street because you ain't got no licence. Stick it down your trouser-leg till you're out in the country, right?'

'Don't worry,' Ernie said. He took the gun and the box of bullets and went out to see what he could kill. He was a big lout of a boy, fifteen years old this birthday. Like his truck-driver father, he had small slitty eyes set very close together near the top of the nose. His mouth was loose, the lips often wet. Brought up in a household where physical violence was an everyday occurrence, he was himself an extremely violent person. Most Saturday afternoons, he and a gang of friends travelled by train or bus to football matches, and if they didn't manage to get into a bloody fight before they returned home, they considered it a wasted day. He took great pleasure in catching small boys after school and twisting their arms behind their backs. Then he would order them to say insulting and filthy things about their own parents.

'Ow! Please don't, Ernie! Please!'

'Say it or I'll twist your arm off!'

They always said it. Then he would give the arm an extra twist and the victim would go off in tears.

Ernie's best friend was called Raymond. He lived four doors away, and he, too, was a big boy for his age. But while Ernie was heavy and loutish, Raymond was tall, slim and muscular.

Outside Raymond's house, Ernie put two fingers in his mouth and gave a long shrill whistle. Raymond came out. 'Look what I got for me birthday,' Ernie said, showing the gun.

'Cripes!' Raymond said. 'We can have some fun with that!'

'Come on, then,' Ernie said. 'We're goin' up to the big field the other side of the lake to get us a rabbit.'

The two boys set off. This was a Saturday morning in May, and the countryside was beautiful around the small village where the boys lived. The chestnut trees were in full flower and the hawthorn was white along the hedges. To reach the big rabbit field, Ernie and Raymond had first to walk down a narrow hedgy lane for half a mile. Then they must cross the railway line, and go round the big lake where wild ducks and moorhens and coots and ring-ouzels lived. Beyond the lake, over the hill and down the other side, lay the rabbit field. This was all private land belonging to Mr Douglas Highton and the lake itself was a sanctuary for waterfowl.

All the way up the lane, they took turns with the gun, potting at small birds in the hedges. Ernie got a bullfinch and a hedge-sparrow. Raymond got a second bullfinch, a whitethroat and a yellowhammer. As each bird was killed, they tied it by the legs to a line of string. Raymond never went anywhere without a big ball of string in his jacket pocket, and a knife. Now they had five little birds dangling on the line of string.

'You know something,' Raymond said. 'We can eat these.'

'Don't talk so daft,' Ernie said. 'There's not enough meat on one of those to feed a woodlouse.'

'There is, too,' Raymond said. 'The Frenchies eat 'em and so do the Eyeties. Mr Sanders told us about it in class. He said the Frenchies and the Eyeties put up nets and catch 'em by the million and then they eat 'em.'

'All right, then,' Ernie said. 'Let's see 'ow many we can get. Then we'll take 'em 'ome and put 'em in the rabbit stew.'

As they progressed up the lane, they shot at every little bird they saw. By the time they got to the railway line, they had fourteen small birds dangling on the line of string.

'Hey!' whispered Ernie, pointing with a long arm. 'Look over there!'

There was a group of trees and bushes alongside the railway line, and beside one of the bushes stood a small boy. He was looking up into the branches of an old tree through a pair of binoculars.

'You know who that is?' Raymond whispered back. 'It's that little twerp Watson.'

'You're right!' Ernie whispered. 'It's Watson, the scum of the earth!'

Peter Watson was always the enemy. Ernie and Raymond detested him because he was nearly everything that they were not. He had a small frail body. His face was freckled and he wore spectacles with thick lenses. He was a brilliant pupil, already in the senior class at school although he was only thirteen. He loved music and played the piano well. He was no good at games. He was quiet and polite. His clothes, although patched and darned, were always clean. And his father did not drive a truck or work in a factory. He worked in the bank.

'Let's give the little perisher a fright,' Ernie whispered.

The two bigger boys crept up close to the small boy, who didn't see them because he still had binoculars to his eyes.

''*Ands up!*' shouted Ernie, pointing the gun.

Peter Watson jumped. He lowered the binoculars and stared through his spectacles at the two intruders.

'Go on!' Ernie shouted. 'Stick 'em up!'

'I wouldn't point that gun if I were you,' Peter Watson said.

'*We're* givin' the orders round 'ere!' Ernie said.

'So stick 'em up,' Raymond said, 'unless you want a slug in the guts!'

Peter Watson stood quite still, holding the binoculars in front of him with both hands. He looked at Raymond. Then he looked at Ernie. He was not afraid, but he knew better than to play the fool with these two. He had suffered a good deal from their attentions over the years.

'What do you want?' he asked.

'*I want you to stick 'em up!*' Ernie yelled at him. 'Can't you understand English?'

Peter Watson didn't move.

'I'll count to five,' Ernie said. 'And if they're not up by then, you get it in the guts. One . . . Two . . . Three . . .'

Peter Watson raised his arms slowly above his head. It was the only sensible thing to do. Raymond stepped forwards and snatched the binoculars from his hands. 'What's this?' he snapped. 'Who you spyin' on?'

'Nobody.'

'Don't lie, Watson. Them things is used for spyin'! I'll bet you was spyin' on us! That's right, ain't it? Confess it!'

'I certainly wasn't spying on you.'

'Give 'im a clip over the ear,' Ernie said. 'Teach 'im not to lie to us.'

'I'll do that in a minute,' Raymond said. 'I'm just workin' meself up.'

Peter Watson considered the possibility of trying to escape. All he could do would be to turn and run, and that was pointless. They'd catch him in seconds. And if he shouted for help, there was no one to hear him. All he could do, therefore, was to keep calm and try to talk his way out of the situation.

'Keep them 'ands up!' Ernie barked, waving the barrel of the gun gently from side to side the way he had seen it done by gangsters on the telly. 'Go on, laddie, reach!'

Peter did as he was told.

'So 'oo was you spyin' on?' Raymond asked. 'Out with it!'

'I was watching a green woodpecker,' Peter said.

'A what?'

'A male green woodpecker. He was tapping the trunk of that old dead tree, searching for grubs.'

'Where is 'ee?' Ernie snapped, raising his gun. 'I'll 'ave 'im!'

'No, you won't,' Peter said, looking at the string of tiny birds slung over Raymond's shoulder. 'He flew off the moment you shouted. Woodpeckers are extremely timid.'

'What you watchin' 'im for?' Raymond asked suspiciously. 'What's the point? Don't you 'ave nothin' better to do?'

'It's fun watching birds,' Peter said. 'It's a lot more fun than shooting them.'

'Why, you cheeky little bleeder!' Ernie cried. 'So you don't like us shootin' birds, eh? Is that what you're sayin'?'

'I think it's absolutely pointless.'

'You don't like anything we do, isn't that right?' Raymond said.

Peter didn't answer.

'Well, let me tell *you* something,' Raymond went on. 'We don't like anything you do either.'

Peter's arms were beginning to ache. He decided to take a risk. Slowly, he lowered them to his sides.

'Up!' yelled Ernie. 'Get 'em up!'

'What if I refuse?'

'Blimey! You got a ruddy nerve, ain't you?' Ernie said. 'I'm tellin' you for the last time, if you don't stick 'em up I'll pull the trigger!'

'That would be a criminal act,' Peter said. 'It would be a case for the police.'

'And you'd be a case for the 'ospital!' Ernie said.

'Go ahead and shoot,' Peter said. 'Then they'll send you to Borstal. That's prison.'

He saw Ernie hesitate.

'You're really askin' for it, ain't you?' Raymond said.

'I'm simply asking to be left alone,' Peter said. 'I haven't done you any harm.'

'You're a stuck-up little squirt,' Ernie said. 'That's exactly what you are, a stuck-up little squirt.'

Raymond leaned over and whispered something in Ernie's ear. Ernie listened intently. Then he slapped his thigh and said, 'I like it! It's a great idea!'

Ernie placed his gun on the ground and advanced upon the small boy. He grabbed him and threw him to the ground. Raymond took the roll of string from his pocket and cut off a length of it. Together, they forced the boy's arms in front of him and tied his wrists together tight.

'Now the legs,' Raymond said. Peter struggled and received a punch in the stomach. That winded him and he lay still. Next, they tied his ankles together with more string. He was now trussed up like a chicken and completely helpless.

Ernie picked up his gun, and then, with his other hand, he grabbed one of Peter's arms. Raymond grabbed the other arm and together they began to drag the boy over the grass towards the railway lines.

Peter kept absolutely quiet. Whatever it was they were up to, talking to them wasn't going to help matters.

They dragged their victim down the embankment and on to the railway lines themselves. Then one took the arms and the other the feet and they lifted him up and laid him down again lengthwise right between two lines.

'You're mad!' Peter said. 'You can't do this!'

''Oo says we can't? This is just a little lesson we're teachin' you not to be cheeky.'

'More string,' Ernie said.

Raymond produced the ball of string and the two larger boys now proceeded to tie the victim down in such a way that he couldn't wriggle away from between the rails. They did this by looping string around each of his arms and then threading the string under the rails on either side. They did the same with his middle body and his ankles. When they had finished, Peter Watson was strung down helpless and virtually immobile between the rails. The only parts of his body he could move to any extent were his head and feet.

Ernie and Raymond stepped back to survey their handiwork. 'We done a nice job,' Ernie said.

'There's trains every 'arf 'our on this line,' Raymond said. 'We ain't gonna 'ave long to wait.'

'This is murder!' cried the small boy lying between the rails.

'No it ain't,' Raymond told him. 'It ain't anything of the sort.'

'Let me go! Please let me go! I'll be killed if a train comes along!'

'If you *are* killed, sonny boy,' Ernie said, 'it'll be your own ruddy fault and I'll tell you why. Because if you lift your 'ead up like you're doin' now, then you've 'ad it, chum! You keep down flat and you might just possibly get away with it. On the other 'and, you might not because I ain't exactly sure 'ow much clearance them trains've got underneath. You 'appen to know, Raymond, 'ow much clearance them trains got underneath?'

'Very little,' Raymond said. 'They're built ever so close to the ground.'

'Might be enough and it might not,' Ernie said.

'Let's put it this way,' Raymond said. 'It'd probably just about be enough for an *ordinary* person like me or you, Ernie. But Mister Watson 'ere I'm not so sure about and I'll tell you why.'

'Tell me,' Ernie said, egging him on.

'Mister Watson 'ere's got an extra big 'ead, that's why. 'Ee's so flippin' big-'eaded I personally think the bottom bit of the train's goin' to scrape 'im whatever 'appens. I'm not saying it's goin' to take 'is 'ead off, mind you. In fact, I'm pretty sure it ain't goin' to do that. But it's goin' to give 'is face a good old scrapin' over. You can be quite sure of that.'

'I think you're right,' Ernie said.

'It don't do,' Raymond said, 'to 'ave a great big swollen 'ead full of brains if you're lyin' on the railway line with a train comin' towards you. That's right, ain't it, Ernie?'

'That's right,' Ernie said.

The two bigger boys climbed back up the embankment and sat on the grass behind some bushes. Ernie produced a pack of cigarettes and they both lit up.

Peter Watson, lying helpless between the rails, realized now that they were not going to release him. These were dangerous, crazy boys. They lived for the moment and never considered the consequences. I must try to keep calm and think, Peter told himself. He lay there, quite still, weighing his chances. His chances were good. The highest part of his head was his nose. He estimated the end of his nose was sticking up about four inches above the rails. Was that too much? He wasn't quite sure what clearance these modern diesels had above the ground. It certainly wasn't very much. The back of his head was resting upon loose gravel in between two sleepers. He must try to burrow down a little into the gravel. So he began to wriggle his head from side to side, pushing the gravel away and gradually making for himself a small indentation, a hole in the gravel. In the end, he reckoned he had lowered his head an extra two inches. That would do for the head. But what about the feet? They were sticking up, too. He took care of that by swinging the two tied-together feet over to one side so they lay almost flat.

He waited for the train to come.

Would the driver see him? It was very unlikely, for this was the main line, London, Doncaster, York, Newcastle and Scotland, and they used huge long engines in which the driver sat in a cab way back and kept an eye open only for the signals. Along this stretch of the track trains travelled around eighty miles an hour. Peter knew that. He had sat on the bank many times watching them. When he was younger, he used to keep a record of their numbers in a little book, and sometimes the engines had names written on their sides in gold letters.

Either way, he told himself, it was going to be a terrifying business. The noise would be deafening, and the swish of the eighty-mile-an-hour wind wouldn't be much fun either. He wondered for a moment whether there would be any kind of vacuum created underneath the train as it rushed over him, sucking him upwards. There might well be. So whatever happened, he must concentrate everything upon pressing his entire body against the ground. Don't go limp. Keep stiff and tense and press down into the ground.

'How're you doin', rat-face!' one of them called out to him from the bushes above. 'What's it like waitin' for the execution?'

He decided not to answer. He watched the blue sky above his head where a single cumulus cloud was drifting slowly from left to right. And to keep his mind off the thing that was going to happen soon, he played a game that his father had taught him long ago on a hot summer's day when they were lying on their backs in the grass above the cliffs at Beachy Head. The game was to look for strange faces in the folds and shadows and billows of a cumulus cloud. If you looked hard enough, his father had said, you would always find a face of some sort up there. Peter let his eyes travel slowly over the cloud. In one place, he found a one-eyed man with a beard. In another, there was a long-chinned laughing witch. An aeroplane came across the cloud travelling from east to west. It was a small high-winged monoplane with a red fuselage. An old Piper Cub, he thought it was. He watched it until it disappeared.

And then, quite suddenly, he heard a curious little vibrating sound coming from the rails on either side of him. It was very soft, this sound, scarcely audible, a tiny little humming, thrumming whisper that seemed to be coming along the rails from far away.

That's a train, he told himself.

The vibrating along the rails grew louder, then louder still. He raised his head and looked down the long and absolutely straight railway line that stretched away for a mile or more into the distance. It was then that he saw the train. At first it was only a speck, a faraway black dot, but in those few seconds that he kept his head raised, the dot grew bigger and bigger, and it began to take shape, and soon it was no longer a dot but the big, square, blunt front-end of a diesel express. Peter dropped his head and pressed it down hard into the small hole he had dug for it in the gravel. He swung his feet over to one side. He shut his eyes tight and tried to sink his body into the ground.

The train came over him like an explosion. It was as though a gun had gone off in his head. And with the explosion came a tearing, screaming wind that was like a hurricane blowing down his nostrils and into his lungs. The noise was shattering. The wind choked him. He felt as if he were being eaten alive and swallowed up in the belly of a screaming murderous monster.

And then it was over. The train had gone. Peter opened his eyes and saw the blue sky and the big white cloud still drifting overhead. It was all over now and he had done it. He had survived.

'It missed 'im,' said a voice.

'What a pity,' said another voice.

He glanced sideways and saw the two large louts standing over him.

'Cut 'im loose,' Ernie said.

Raymond cut the strings binding him to the rails on either side.

'Undo 'is feet so 'ee can walk, but keep 'is 'ands tied,' Ernie said.

Raymond cut the strings around his ankles.

'Get up,' Ernie said.

Peter got to his feet.

'You're still a prisoner, matey,' Ernie said.

'What about them rabbits?' Raymond asked. 'I thought we was goin' to try for a few rabbits?'

'Plenty of time for that,' Ernie answered. 'I just thought we'd push the little bleeder into the lake on the way.'

'Good,' Raymond said. 'Cool 'im down.'

'You've had your fun,' Peter Waston said. 'Why don't you let me go now?'

'Because you're a prisoner,' Ernie said. 'And you ain't just no ordinary prisoner neither. You're a spy. And you know what 'appens to spies when they get caught, don't you? They get put up against the wall and shot.'

Peter didn't say any more after that. There was no point at all in provoking those two. The less he said to them and the less he resisted them, the more chance he would have of escaping injury. He had no doubt whatsoever that in their present mood they were capable of doing him quite serious bodily harm. He knew for a fact that Ernie had once broken little Wally Simpson's arm after school and Wally's parents had gone to the police. He had also heard Raymond boasting about what he called 'putting the boot in' at the football matches they went to. This, he understood, meant kicking someone in the face or body when he was lying on the ground. They were hooligans, these two, and from what Peter read in his father's newspaper nearly every day, they were not by any means on their own. It seemed the whole country was full of hooligans. They wrecked the interiors of trains, they fought pitched battles in the streets with knives and bicycle chains and metal clubs, they attacked pedestrains, especially other young boys walking alone, and they smashed up roadside cafés. Ernie and Raymond, though perhaps not quite yet fully qualified hooligans, were most definitely on their way.

Therefore, Peter told himself, he must continue to be passive. Do not insult them. Do not aggravate them in any way. And above all, do not try to take them on physically. Then, hopefully, in the end, they might become bored with this nasty little game and go off to shoot rabbits.

The two larger boys had each taken hold of one of Peter's arms and they were marching him across the next field towards the lake. The prisoner's wrists were still tied together in front of him. Ernie carried the gun in his spare hand. Raymond carried the binoculars he had taken from Peter. They came to the lake.

The lake was beautiful on this golden May morning. It was a long and fairly narrow lake with tall willow trees growing here and there along its banks. In the middle, the water was clear and clean, but nearer to the land there was a forest of reeds and bulrushes.

Ernie and Raymond marched their prisoner to the edge of the lake and there they stopped.

'Now then,' Ernie said. 'What I suggest is this. You take 'is arms and I take 'is legs and we'll swing the little per-isher one two three as far out as we can into them nice muddy reeds. 'Ow's that?'

'I like it,' Raymond said. 'And leave 'is 'ands tied together, right?'

'Right,' Ernie said. "Ow's that with you, snot-nose?'

'If that's what you're going to do, I can't very well stop you,' Peter said, trying to keep his voice cool and calm.

'Just you try and stop us,' Ernie said, grinning, 'and then see what 'appens to you.'

'One last question,' Peter said. 'Did you ever take on somebody your own size?'

The moment he said it, he knew he had made a mistake. He saw the flush coming to Ernie's cheeks and there was a dangerous little spark dancing in his small black eyes.

Luckily, at that very moment, Raymond saved the situation. 'Hey! Lookit that bird swimmin' in the reeds over there!' he shouted, pointing. 'Let's 'ave 'im!'

It was a mallard drake, with a curvy spoon-shaped yellow beak and a head of emerald green with a white ring round its neck. 'Now those you really *can* eat,' Raymond went on. 'It's a wild duck.'

'I'll 'ave 'im!' Ernie cried. He let go of the prisoner's arm and lifted the gun to his shoulder.

'This is a bird sanctuary,' Peter said.

'A what?' Ernie asked, lowering the gun.

'Nobody shoots birds here. It's strictly forbidden.'

"Oo says it's forbidden?'

'The owner, Mr Douglas Highton.'

'You must be joking,' Ernie said and he raised the gun again. He fired. The duck crumpled in the water.

'Go get 'im,' Ernie said to Peter. 'Cut 'is 'ands free, Raymond, 'cause then 'ee can be our flippin' gun-dog and fetch the birds after we shoot 'em.'

Raymond took out his knife and cut the string binding the small boy's wrists.

'Go on!' Ernie snapped. 'Go get 'im!'

The killing of the beautiful duck had disturbed Peter very much. 'I refuse,' he said.

Ernie hit him across the face hard with his open hand. Peter didn't fall down, but a small trickle of blood began running out of one nostril.

'You dirty little perisher!' Ernie said. 'You just try refusin' me one more time and I'm goin' to make you a promise. And the promise is like this. You refuse me just one more time and I'm goin' to knock out every single one of them shiny white front teeth of yours, top and bottom. You understand that?'

Peter said nothing.

'Answer me!' Ernie barked. 'Do you understand that?'

'Yes,' Peter said quietly. 'I understand.'

'Get on with it, then!' Ernie shouted.

Peter walked down the bank, into the muddy water, through the reeds, and picked up the duck. He brought it back and Raymond took it from him and tied string around its legs.

'Now we got a retriever dog with us, let's see if we can't get us a few more of them ducks,' Ernie said. He strolled along the bank, gun in hand, searching the reeds. Suddenly he stopped. He crouched. He put a finger to his lips and said, 'Sshh!'

Raymond went over to join him. Peter stood a few yards away, his trousers covered in mud up to the knees.

'Lookit in there!' Ernie whispered, pointing into a dense patch of bulrushes. 'D'you see what I see?'

'Holy cats!' cried Raymond. 'What a beauty!'

Peter, peering from a little further away into the rushes, saw at once what they were looking at. It was a swan, a magnificent white swan sitting serenely upon her nest. The nest itself was a huge pile of reeds and rushes that rose up about two feet above the waterline, and upon the top of all this the swan was sitting like a great white lady of the lake. Her head was turned towards the boys on the bank, alert and watchful.

''Ow about *that*?' Ernie said. 'That's better'n ducks, ain't it?'

'You think you can get 'er?' Raymond said.

'Of course I can get 'er. I'll drill a 'ole right through 'er noggin!'

Peter felt a wild rage beginning to build up inside him. He walked up to the two bigger boys. 'I wouldn't shoot that swan if I were you,' he said, trying to keep his voice calm. 'Swans are the most protected birds in England.'

'And what's that got to do with it?' Ernie asked him, sneering.

'And I'll tell you something else,' Peter went on, throwing all caution away. 'Nobody shoots a bird sitting on its nest. Absolutely nobody! She may even have cygnets under her! You just can't do it!'

''Oo says we can't?' Raymond asked, sneering. 'Mister bleedin' snotty-nose Peter Watson, is that the one 'oo says it?'

'The whole country says it,' Peter answered. 'The law says it and the police say it and *everyone* says it!'

'I don't say it!' Ernie said, raising his gun.

'Don't!' screamed Peter. 'Please don't!'

*Crack!* The gun went off. The bullet hit the swan right in the middle of her elegant head and the long white neck collapsed on to the side of the nest.

'Got 'er!' cried Ernie.

'Hot shot!' shouted Raymond.

Ernie turned to Peter who was standing small and white-faced and absolutely rigid. 'Now go get 'er,' he ordered.

Once again, Peter didn't move.

Ernie came up close to the smaller boy and bent down and stuck his face right up to Peter's. 'I'm tellin' you for the last time,' he said, soft and dangerous. 'Go get 'er!'

Tears were running down Peter's face as he went slowly down the bank and entered the water. He waded out to the dead swan and picked it up tenderly with both hands. Underneath it were two tiny cygnets, their bodies covered with yellow down. They were huddling together in the centre of the nest.

'Any eggs?' Ernie shouted from the bank.

'No,' Peter answered. 'Nothing.' There was a chance, he felt, that when the male swan returned, it would continue to feed the young ones on its own if they were left in the nest. He certainly did not want to leave them to the tender mercies of Ernie and Raymond.

Peter carried the dead swan back to the edge of the lake. He placed it on the ground. Then he stood up and faced the two others. His eyes, still wet with tears, were blazing with fury. 'That was a filthy thing to do!' he shouted. 'It was a stupid pointless act of vandalism! You're a couple of ignorant idiots! It's you who ought to be dead instead of the swan! You're not fit to be alive!'

He stood there, as tall as he could stand, splendid in his fury, facing the two taller boys and not caring any longer what they did to him.

Ernie didn't hit him this time. He seemed just a tiny bit taken aback at first by this outburst, but he quickly recovered. And now his loose lips formed themselves into a sly, wet smirk and his small close-together eyes began to glint in a most malicious manner. 'So you like swans, is that right?' he asked softly.

'I like swans and I hate you!' Peter cried.

'And am I right in thinkin',' Ernie went on, still smirking, 'am I absolutely right in thinkin' that you wished this old swan down 'ere were alive instead of dead?'

'That's a stupid question!' Peter shouted.

''Ee needs a clip over the ear-'ole,' Raymond said.

'Wait,' Ernie said. 'I'm doin' this exercise.' He turned back to Peter. 'So if I could make this swan come alive and go flyin' round the sky all over again, then you'd be 'appy. Right?'

'That's another stupid question!' Peter cried out. 'Who d'you think you are?'

'I'll tell you 'oo I am,' Ernie said. 'I'm a magic man, that's 'oo I am. And just to make you 'appy and contented,

I am about to do a magic trick that'll make this dead swan come alive and go flyin' all over the sky once again.'

'Rubbish!' Peter said. 'I'm going.' He turned and started to walk away.

'Grab 'im!' Ernie said.

Raymond grabbed him.

'Leave me alone!' Peter cried out.

Raymond slapped him on the cheek, hard. 'Now, now,' he said. 'Don't fight with auntie, not unless you want to get 'urt.'

'Gimme your knife,' Ernie said, holding out his hand. Raymond gave him his knife.

Ernie knelt down beside the dead swan and stretched out one of its enormous wings. 'Watch this,' he said.

'What's the big idea?' Raymond asked.

'Wait and see,' Ernie said. And now, using the knife, he proceeded to sever the great white wing from the swan's body. There is a joint in the bone where the wing meets the side of the bird, and Ernie located this and slid the knife into the joint and cut through the tendon. The knife was very sharp and it cut well, and soon the wing came away all in one piece.

Ernie turned the swan over and severed the other wing.

'String,' he said, holding out his hand to Raymond.

Raymond, who was grasping Peter by the arm, was watching fascinated. 'Where'd you learn 'ow to butcher up a bird like that?' he asked.

'With chickens,' Ernie said. 'We used to nick chickens from up at Stevens Farm and cut 'em up into chicken parts and flog 'em to a shop in Aylesbury. Gimme the string.'

Raymond gave him the ball of string. Ernie cut off six pieces, each about a yard long.

There are a series of strong bones running along the top edge of a swan's wing, and Ernie took one of the wings and started tying one end of the bits of string all the way along the top edge of the great wing. When he had done this, he lifted the wing with the six string ends dangling from it and said to Peter, 'Stick out your arm.'

'You're absolutely mad!' the smaller boy shouted. 'You're demented!'

'Make 'im stick it out,' Ernie said to Raymond.

Raymond held up a clenched fist in front of Peter's face and dabbed it gently against his nose. 'You see this,' he said. 'Well I'm goin' to smash you right in the kisser with it unless you do exactly as you're told, see? Now, stick out your arm, there's a good little boy.'

Peter felt his resistance collapsing. He couldn't hold out against these people any longer. For a few seconds, he stared at Ernie. Ernie with the tiny close-together black eyes gave the impression he would be capable of doing just about anything if he got really angry. Ernie, Peter felt at that moment, might quite easily kill a person if he were to lose his temper. Ernie, the dangerous backward child, was playing games now and it would be very unwise to spoil his fun. Peter held out an arm.

Ernie then proceeded to tie the six string ends one by one to Peter's arm, and when he had finished, the white wing of the swan was securely attached along the entire length of the arm itself.

'Ow's that, eh?' Ernie said, stepping back and surveying his work.

'Now the other one,' Raymond said, catching on to what Ernie was doing. 'You can't expect 'im to go flyin' round the sky with only one wing, can you?'

'Second wing comin' up,' Ernie said. He knelt down again and tied six more lengths of string to the top bones of the second wing. Then he stood up again. 'Let's 'ave the other arm,' he said. Peter, feeling sick and ridiculous, held out his other arm. Ernie strapped the wing tightly along the length of it.

'Now!' Ernie cried, clapping his hands and dancing a little jig on the grass. 'Now we got ourselves a real live swan all over again! Didn't I tell you I was a magic man? Didn't I tell you I was goin' to do a magic trick and make this dead swan come alive and go flyin' all over the sky? Didn't I tell you that?'

Peter stood there in the sunshine beside the lake on this beautiful May morning, the enormous, limp and slightly bloodied wings dangling grotesquely at his sides. 'Have you finished?' he said.

'Swans don't talk,' Ernie said. 'Keep your flippin' beak shut! And save your energy, laddie, because you're goin' to need all the strength and energy you got when it comes to flyin' round in the sky.' Ernie picked up his gun from the ground, then he grabbed Peter by the back of the neck with his free hand and said, 'March!'

They marched along the bank of the lake until they

came to a tall and graceful willow tree. There they halted. The tree was a weeping willow, and the long branches hung down from a great height and almost touched the surface of the lake.

'And now the magic swan is goin' to show us a bit of magic flyin',' Ernie announced. 'So what you're goin' to do, Mister Swan, is to climb up to the very top of this tree, and when you get there you're goin' to spread out your wings like a clever little swannee-swan-swan and you're goin' to take off!'

'Fantastic!' cried Raymond. 'Terrific! I like it very much!'

'So do I,' Ernie said. 'Because now we're goin' to find out just exactly 'ow clever this clever little swannee-swan-swan really is. 'Ee's terribly clever at school, we all know that, and 'ee's top of the class and everything else that's lovely, but let's see just exactly 'ow clever 'ee is when 'ee's at the top of the tree! Right, Mister Swan?' He gave Peter a push towards the tree.

How much further could this madness go? Peter wondered. He was beginning to feel a little mad himself, as though nothing was real any more and none of it was actually happening. But the thought of being high up in the tree and out of reach of these hooligans at last was something that appealed to him greatly. When he was up there, he could stay up there. He doubted very much if they would bother to come up after him. And even if they did, he could surely climb away from them along a thin limb that would not take the weight of two people.

The tree was a fairly easy one to climb, with several low branches to give him a start up. He began climbing. The huge white wings dangling from his arms kept getting in the way, but it didn't matter. What mattered now to Peter was that every inch upwards was another inch away from his tormentors below. He had never been a great one for tree-climbing and he wasn't especially good at it, but nothing in the world was going to stop him from getting to the top of this one. And once he was there, he thought it unlikely they would even be able to see him because of the leaves.

'Higher!' shouted Ernie's voice. 'Keep goin'!'

Peter kept going, and eventually he arrived at a point where it was impossible to go higher. His feet were now standing on a branch that was about as thick as a person's wrist, and this particular branch reached far out over the lake and then curved gracefully downwards. All the branches above him were very thin and whippy, but the one he was holding on to with his hands was quite strong enough for the purpose. He stood there, resting after the climb. He looked down for the first time. He was very high up, at least fifty feet. But he couldn't see the two boys. They were no longer standing at the base of the tree. Was it possible they had gone away at last?

'All right, Mister Swan!' came the dreaded voice of Ernie. 'Now listen carefully!'

The two of them had walked some distance away from the tree to a point where they had a clear view of the small boy at the top. Looking down at them now, Peter realized how very sparse and slender the leaves of a willow tree were. They gave him almost no cover at all.

'Listen carefully, Mister Swan!' the voice was shouting.

'Start walking out along that branch you're standin' on! Keep goin' till you're right over the nice muddy water! Then you take off!'

Peter didn't move. He was fifty feet above them now and they weren't ever going to reach him again. From down below, there was a long silence. It lasted maybe half a minute. He kept his eyes on the two distant figures in the field. They were standing quite still, looking up at him.

'All right then, Mister Swan!' came Ernie's voice again. 'I'm gonna count to ten, right? And if you ain't spread them wings and flown away by then, I'm gonna shoot you down instead with this little gun! And that'll make two swans I've knocked off today instead of one! So here we go, Mister Swan! One! . . . Two! . . . Three! . . . Four! . . . Five! . . . Six! . . .'

Peter remained still. Nothing would make him move from now on.

'Seven! . . . Eight! . . . Nine! . . . Ten!'

Peter saw the gun coming up to the shoulder. It was pointing straight at him. Then he heard the *crack* of the rifle and the *zip* of the bullet as it whistled past his head. It was a frightening thing. But he still didn't move. He could see Ernie loading the gun with another bullet.

'Last chance!' yelled Ernie. 'The next one's gonna get you!'

Peter stayed put. He waited. He watched the boy who was standing among the buttercups in the meadow far below with the other boy beside him. The gun came up once again to the shoulder.

This time he heard the *crack* at the same instant the

bullet hit him in the thigh. There was no pain, but the force of it was devastating. It was as though someone had whacked him on the leg with a sledgehammer, and it knocked both feet off the branch he was standing on. He scrabbled with his hands to hang on. The small branch he was holding on to bent over and split.

Some people, when they have taken too much and have been driven beyond the point of endurance, simply crumble and give up. There are others, though they are not many, who will for some reason always be unconquerable. You meet them in time of war and also in time of peace. They have an indomitable spirit and nothing, neither pain nor torture nor threat of death, will cause them to give up.

Little Peter Watson was one of these. And as he fought and scrabbled to prevent himself from falling out of the top of that tree, it came to him suddenly that he was going to win. He looked up and he saw a light shining over the waters of the lake that was of such brilliance and beauty he was unable to look away from it. The light was beckoning him, drawing him on, and he dived towards the light and spread his wings.

Three different people reported seeing a great white swan circling over the village that morning, a schoolteacher called Emily Mead, a man who was replacing some tiles on the roof of the chemist's shop whose name was William Eyles, and a boy called John Underwood who was flying his model aeroplane in a nearby field.

And that morning, Mrs Watson, who was washing up some dishes in her kitchen sink, happened to glance up through the window at the exact moment when something huge and white came flopping down on to the lawn in her back garden. She rushed outside. She went down on her knees beside the small crumpled figure of her only son. 'Oh, my darling!' she cried, near to hysterics and hardly believing what she saw. 'My darling boy! What happened to you?'

'My leg hurts,' Peter said, opening his eyes. Then he fainted.

'It's bleeding!' she cried and she picked him up and carried him inside. Quickly she phoned for the doctor and the ambulance. And while she was waiting for help to come, she fetched a pair of scissors and began cutting the string that held the two great wings of the swan to her son's arms.

# Poison

First published in *Collier's* ( June 1950)

It must have been around midnight when I drove home, and as I approached the gates of the bungalow I switched off the headlamps of the car so the beam wouldn't swing in through the window of the side bedroom and wake Harry Pope. But I needn't have bothered. Coming up the drive I noticed his light was still on, so he was awake anyway – unless perhaps he'd dropped off while reading.

I parked the car and went up the five steps to the balcony, counting each step carefully in the dark so I wouldn't take an extra one which wasn't there when I got to the top. I crossed the balcony, pushed through the screen doors into the house itself and switched on the light in the hall. I went across to the door of Harry's room, opened it quietly and looked in.

He was lying on the bed and I could see he was awake. But he didn't move. He didn't even turn his head towards me, but I heard him say, 'Timber, Timber, come here.'

He spoke slowly, whispering each word carefully, separately, and I pushed the door right open and started to go quickly across the room.

'Stop. Wait a moment, Timber.' I could hardly hear what he was saying. He seemed to be straining enormously to get the words out.

'What's the matter, Harry?'

'Sshhh!' he whispered. 'Sshhh! For God's sake, don't make a noise. Take your shoes off before you come nearer. *Please* do as I say, Timber.'

The way he was speaking reminded me of George Barling after he got shot in the stomach when he stood leaning against a crate containing a spare aeroplane engine, holding both hands on his stomach and saying things about the German pilot in just the same hoarse straining half-whisper Harry was using now.

'Quickly, Timber, but take your shoes off first.'

I couldn't understand about taking off the shoes but I figured that if he was as ill as he sounded I'd better humour him, so I bent down and removed the shoes and left them in the middle of the floor. Then I went over to his bed.

'Don't touch the bed! For God's sake, don't touch the bed!' He was still speaking like he'd been shot in the stomach and I could see him lying there on his back with a single sheet covering three-quarters of his body. He was wearing a pair of pyjamas with blue, brown and white stripes, and he was sweating terribly. It was a hot night and I was sweating a little myself, but not like Harry. His whole face was wet and the pillow around his head was sodden with moisture. It looked like a bad go of malaria to me.

'What is it, Harry?'

'A krait,' he said.

'A *krait*! Oh my God! Where'd it bite you? How long ago?'

'Shut up,' he whispered.

'Listen, Harry,' I said, and I leaned forward and touched his shoulder. 'We've got to be quick. Come on now, quickly, tell me where it bit you.' He was lying there very still and tense as though he was holding on to himself hard because of sharp pain.

'I haven't been bitten,' he whispered. 'Not yet. It's on my stomach. Lying there asleep.'

I took a quick pace backwards. I couldn't help it, and I stared at his stomach or rather at the sheet that covered it. The sheet was rumpled in several places and it was impossible to tell if there was anything underneath.

'You don't really mean there's a krait lying on your stomach now?'

'I swear it.'

'How did it get there?' I shouldn't have asked the question because it was easy to see he wasn't fooling. I should have told him to keep quiet.

'I was reading,' Harry said, and he spoke very slowly, taking each word in turn and speaking it carefully so as not to move the muscles of his stomach. 'Lying on my back reading and I felt something on my chest, behind the book. Sort of tickling. Then out of the corner of my eye saw this little krait sliding over my pyjamas. Small, about ten inches. Knew I mustn't move. Couldn't have anyway. Lay there watching it. Thought it would go over top of the sheet.' Harry paused and was silent for a few moments. His eyes looked down along his body towards the place where the sheet covered his stomach, and I could see he was watching to make sure his whispering wasn't disturbing the thing that lay there.

'There was a fold in the sheet,' he said, speaking more slowly than ever now and so softly I had to lean close to hear him. 'See it, it's still there. It went under that. I could feel it through my pyjamas, moving on my stomach. Then it stopped moving and now it's lying there in the warmth. Probably asleep. I've been waiting for you.' He raised his eyes and looked at me.

'How long ago?'

'Hours,' he whispered. 'Hours and bloody hours and hours. I can't keep still much longer. I've been wanting to cough.'

There was not much doubt about the truth of Harry's story. As a matter of fact, it wasn't a surprising thing for a krait to do. They hang around people's houses and they go for the warm places. The surprising thing was that Harry hadn't been bitten. The bite is quite deadly, except sometimes when you catch it at once and they kill a fair number of people each year in Bengal, mostly in the villages.

'All right, Harry,' I said, and now I was whispering too. 'Don't move and don't talk any more unless you have to. You know it won't bite unless it's frightened. We'll fix it in no time.'

I went softly out of the room in my stocking feet and fetched a small sharp knife from the kitchen. I put it in my trouser pocket ready to use instantly in case something went wrong while we were still thinking out a plan. If Harry coughed or moved or did something to frighten the krait and got bitten, I was going to be ready to cut the bitten place and try to suck the venom out. I came back to the bedroom and Harry was still lying there very quiet and sweating all over his face. His eyes followed me as I moved across the room to his bed and I could see he was wondering what I'd been up to. I stood beside him, trying to think of the best thing to do.

'Harry,' I said, and now when I spoke I put my mouth almost on his ear so I wouldn't have to raise my voice above the softest whisper, 'I think the best thing to do is for me to draw the sheet back very, very gently. Then we could have a look first. I think I could do that without disturbing it.'

'Don't be a damn fool.' There was no expression in his voice. He spoke each word too slowly, too carefully, and too softly for that. The expression was in the eyes and around the corners of the mouth.

'Why not?'

'The light would frighten him. It's dark under there now.'

'Then how about whipping the sheet back quick and brushing it off before it has time to strike?'

'Why don't you get a doctor?' Harry said. The way he looked at me told me I should have thought of that myself in the first place.

'A doctor. Of course. That's it. I'll get Ganderbai.'

I tiptoed out to the hall, looked up Ganderbai's number in the book, lifted the phone and told the operator to hurry.

'Dr Ganderbai,' I said. 'This is Timber Woods.'

'Hello, Mr Woods. You not in bed yet?'

'Look, could you come round at once? And bring serum – for a krait bite.'

'Who's been bitten?' The question came so sharply it was like a small explosion in my ear.

'No one. No one yet. But Harry Pope's in bed and he's got one lying on his stomach – asleep under the sheet on his stomach.'

For about three seconds there was silence on the line. Then speaking slowly, not like an explosion now but slowly, precisely, Ganderbai said, 'Tell him to keep quite still. He is not to move or to talk. Do you understand?'

'Of course.'

'I'll come at once!' He rang off and I went back to the bedroom. Harry's eyes watched me as I walked across to his bed.

'Ganderbai's coming. He said for you to lie still.'

'What in God's name does he think I'm doing!'

'Look, Harry, he said no talking. Absolutely no talking. Either of us.'

'Why don't you shut up then?' When he said this, one side of his mouth started twitching with rapid little downward movements that continued for a while after he finished speaking. I took out my handkerchief and very gently I wiped the sweat off his face and neck, and I could feel the slight twitching of the muscle – the one he used for smiling – as my fingers passed over it with the handkerchief.

I slipped out to the kitchen, got some ice from the icebox, rolled it up in a napkin, and began to crush it small. That business of the mouth, I didn't like that. Or the way he talked, either. I carried the ice pack back to the bedroom and laid it across Harry's forehead.

'Keep you cool.'

He screwed up his eyes and drew breath sharply

through his teeth. 'Take it away,' he whispered. 'Make me cough.' His smiling-muscle began to twitch again.

The beam of a headlamp shone through the window as Ganderbai's car swung around to the front of the bungalow. I went out to meet him, holding the ice pack with both hands.

'How is it?' Ganderbai asked, but he didn't stop to talk, he walked on past me across the balcony and through the screen doors into the hall. 'Where is he? Which room?'

He put his bag down on a chair in the hall and followed me into Harry's room. He was wearing soft-soled bedroom slippers and he walked across the floor noiselessly, delicately, like a careful cat. Harry watched him out of the sides of his eyes. When Ganderbai reached the bed he looked down at Harry and smiled, confident and reassuring, nodding his head to tell Harry it was a simple matter and he was not to worry but just to leave it to Dr Ganderbai. Then he turned and went back to the hall and I followed him.

'First thing is to try to get some serum into him,' he said, and he opened his bag and started to make preparations. 'Intravenously. But I must do it neatly. Don't want to make him flinch.'

We went into the kitchen and he sterilized a needle. He had a hypodermic syringe in one hand and a small bottle in the other and he stuck the needle through the rubber top of the bottle and began drawing a pale yellow liquid up into the syringe by pulling out the plunger. Then he handed the syringe to me.

'Hold that till I ask for it.'

He picked up the bag and together we returned to the room. Harry's eyes were bright now and wide open. Ganderbai bent over Harry and, very cautiously, like a man handling sixteenth-century lace, he rolled up the pyjama sleeve to the elbow without moving the arm. I noticed he stood well away from the bed.

He whispered, 'I'm going to give you an injection. Serum. Just a prick but try not to move. Don't tighten your stomach muscles. Let them go limp.'

Harry looked at the syringe.

Ganderbai took a piece of red rubber tubing from his bag and slid one end under and up and around Harry's biceps; then he tied the tubing tight with a knot. He sponged a small area of the bare forearm with alcohol, handed the swab to me and took the syringe from my hand. He held it up to the light, squinting at the calibrations, squinting out some of the yellow fluid. I stood still beside him, watching. Harry was watching too and sweating all over his face so it shone like it was smeared thick with face cream melting on his skin and running down on to the pillow.

I could see the blue vein on the inside of Harry's forearm, swollen now because of the tourniquet, and then I saw the needle above the vein, Ganderbai holding the syringe almost flat against the arm, sliding the needle in sideways through the skin into the blue vein, sliding it slowly but so firmly it went in smooth as into cheese. Harry looked at the ceiling and closed his eyes and opened them again, but he didn't move.

When it was finished Ganderbai leaned forward,

putting his mouth close to Harry's ear. 'Now you'll be all right even if you *are* bitten. But don't move. Please don't move. I'll be back in a moment.'

He picked up his bag and went out to the hall and I followed.

'Is he safe now?' I asked.

'No.'

'How safe is he?'

The little Indian doctor stood there in the hall rubbing his lower lip.

'It must give some protection, mustn't it?' I asked.

He turned away and walked to the screen doors that led on to the veranda. I thought he was going through them, but he stopped this side of the doors and stood looking out into the night.

'Isn't the serum very good?' I asked.

'Unfortunately not,' he answered, without turning round. 'It might save him. It might not. I am trying to think of something else to do.'

'Shall we draw the sheet back quick and brush it off before it has time to strike?'

'Never! We are not entitled to take a risk.' He spoke sharply and his voice was pitched a little higher than usual.

'We can't very well leave him lying there,' I said. 'He's getting nervous.'

'Please! Please!' he said, turning round, holding both hands up in the air. 'Not so fast, please. This is not a matter to rush into bald-headed.' He wiped his forehead with his handkerchief and stood there, frowning, nibbling his lip.

'You see,' he said at last. 'There is a way to do this. You

know what we must do – we must administer an anaesthetic to the creature where it lies.'

It was a splendid idea.

'It is not safe,' he continued, 'because a snake is cold-
blooded and anaesthetic does not work so well or so quick
with such animals, but it is better than any other thing to
do. We could use ether . . . chloroform . . .' He was speaking slowly and trying to think the thing out while he talked.

'Which shall we use?'

'Chloroform,' he said suddenly. 'Ordinary chloroform.
That is best. Now quick!' He took my arm and pulled me
towards the balcony. 'Drive to my house! By the time you
get there I will have waked up my boy on the telephone
and he will show you my poisons cupboard. Here is the
key of the cupboard. Take a bottle of chloroform. It has
an orange label and the name is printed on it. I stay here
in case anything happens. Be quick now, hurry! No, no,
you don't need your shoes!'

I drove fast and in about fifteen minutes I was back
with the bottle of chloroform. Ganderbai came out of
Harry's room and met me in the hall. 'You got it?' he said.
'Good, good. I just been telling him what we are going to
do. But now we must hurry. It is not easy for him in there
like that all this time. I am afraid he might move.'

He went back to the bedroom and I followed, carrying
the bottle carefully with both hands. Harry was lying on
the bed in precisely the same position as before with the
sweat pouring down his cheeks. His face was white and
wet. He turned his eyes towards me and I smiled at him
and nodded confidently. He continued to look at me. I

raised my thumb, giving him the OK signal. He closed his eyes. Ganderbai was squatting down by the bed, and on the floor beside him was the hollow rubber tube that he had previously used as a tourniquet, and he'd got a small paper funnel fitted into one end of the tube.

He began to pull a little piece of the sheet out from under the mattress. He was working directly in line with Harry's stomach, about eighteen inches from it, and I watched his fingers as they tugged gently at the edge of the sheet. He worked so slowly it was almost impossible to discern any movement either in his fingers or in the sheet that was being pulled.

Finally he succeeded in making an opening under the sheet and he took the rubber tube and inserted one end of it in the opening so that it would slide under the sheet along the mattress towards Harry's body. I do not know how long it took him to slide that tube in a few inches. It may have been twenty minutes, it may have been forty. I never once saw the tube move. I knew it was going in because the visible part of it grew gradually shorter, but I doubted that the krait could have felt even the faintest vibration. Ganderbai himself was sweating now, large pearls of sweat standing out all over his forehead and along his upper lip. But his hands were steady and I noticed that his eyes were watching, not the tube in his hands, but the area of crumpled sheet above Harry's stomach.

Without looking up, he held out a hand to me for the chloroform. I twisted out the ground-glass stopper and put the bottle right into his hand, not letting go till I was sure he had a good hold on it. Then he jerked his head for me to come closer and he whispered, 'Tell him I'm going to soak the mattress and that it will be very cold under his body. He must be ready for that and he must not move. Tell him now.'

I bent over Harry and passed on the message.

'Why doesn't he get on with it?' Harry said.

'He's going to now, Harry. But it'll feel very cold, so be ready for it.'

'Oh God Almighty, get on, get on!' For the first time he raised his voice, and Ganderbai glanced up sharply, watched him for a few seconds, then went back to his business.

Ganderbai poured a few drops of chloroform into the paper funnel and waited while it ran down the tube. Then he poured some more. Then he waited again, and the heavy sickening smell of chloroform spread out over the room bringing with it faint unpleasant memories of white-coated nurses and white surgeons standing in a white room around a long white table. Ganderbai was pouring steadily now and I could see the heavy vapour of the chloroform swirling slowly like smoke above the paper funnel. He paused, held the bottle up to the light, poured one more funnelful and handed the bottle back to me. Slowly he drew out the rubber tube from under the sheet; then he stood up.

The strain of inserting the tube and pouring the chloroform must have been great, and I recollect that when Ganderbai turned and whispered to me, his voice was small and tired. 'We'll give it fifteen minutes. Just to be safe.'

I leaned over to tell Harry. 'We're going to give it fifteen minutes, just to be safe. But it's probably done for already.'

'Then why for God's sake don't you look and see!' Again he spoke loudly and Ganderbai sprang round, his small brown face suddenly very angry. He had almost pure-black eyes and he stared at Harry and Harry's smiling-muscle started to twitch. I took my handkerchief and wiped his wet face, trying to stroke his forehead a little for comfort as I did so.

Then we stood and waited beside the bed, Ganderbai watching Harry's face all the time in a curious intense manner. The little Indian was concentrating all his will-power on keeping Harry quiet. He never once took his eyes from the patient and although he made no sound, he seemed somehow to be shouting at him all the time, say-ing: Now listen, you've got to listen, you're not going to go spoiling this now, d'you hear me, and Harry lay there twitching his mouth, sweating, closing his eyes, opening them, looking at me, at the sheet, at the ceiling, at me again, but never at Ganderbai. Yet somehow Ganderbai was holding him. The smell of chloroform was oppres-sive and it made me feel sick, but I couldn't leave the room now. I had the feeling someone was blowing up a huge balloon and I could see it was going to burst, but I couldn't look away.

At length Ganderbai turned and nodded and I knew he was ready to proceed. 'You go over to the other side of the bed,' he said. 'We will each take one side of the sheet and draw it back together, but very slowly, please, and very quietly.'

'Keep still now, Harry,' I said and I went around to the other side of the bed and took hold of the sheet. Ganderbai stood opposite me, and together we began to draw back the sheet, lifting it up clear of Harry's body, taking it back very slowly, both of us standing well away but at the same time bending forward, trying to peer underneath it. The smell of chloroform was awful. I remember trying to hold my breath and when I couldn't do that any longer I tried to breathe shallow so the stuff wouldn't get into my lungs.

The whole of Harry's chest was visible now, or rather the striped pyjama top which covered it, and then I saw the white cord of his pyjama trousers, neatly tied in a bow. A little farther and I saw a button, a mother-of-pearl button, and that was something I had never had on my pyjamas, a fly button, let alone a mother-of-pearl one. This Harry, I thought, he is very refined. It is odd how one sometimes has frivolous thoughts at exciting moments, and I distinctly remember thinking about Harry being very refined when I saw that button.

Apart from the button there was nothing on his stomach.

We pulled the sheet back faster then, and when we had uncovered his legs and feet we let the sheet drop over the end of the bed on to the floor.

'Don't move,' Ganderbai said. 'Don't move, Mr Pope,' and he began to peer around along the side of Harry's body and under his legs.

'We must be careful,' he said. It may be anywhere. It could be up the leg of his pyjamas.'

When Ganderbai said this, Harry quickly raised his head from the pillow and looked down at his legs. It was the first time he had moved. Then suddenly he jumped up, stood on his bed and shook his legs one after the other violently in the air. At that moment we both thought he had been bitten and Ganderbai was already reaching down into his bag for a scalpel and a tourniquet when Harry ceased his caperings and stood still and looked at the mattress he was standing on and shouted, 'It's not there!'

Ganderbai straightened up and for a moment he too looked at the mattress; then he looked up at Harry. Harry was all right. He hadn't been bitten and now he wasn't going to get bitten and he wasn't going to be killed and everything was fine. But that didn't seem to make anyone feel any better.

'Mr Pope, you are of course *quite* sure you saw it in the first place?' There was a note of sarcasm in Ganderbai's voice that he would never have employed in ordinary circumstances. 'You don't think you might possibly have been dreaming, do you, Mr Pope?' The way Ganderbai was looking at Harry, I realized that the sarcasm was not seriously intended. He was only easing up a bit after the strain.

Harry stood on his bed in his striped pyjamas, glaring at Ganderbai, and the colour began to spread out over his cheeks.

'Are you telling me I'm a liar?' he shouted.

Ganderbai remained absolutely still, watching Harry. Harry took a pace forward on the bed and there was a shining look in his eyes.

'Why, you dirty little Hindu sewer rat!'

'Shut up, Harry!' I said.

'You dirty black –'

'Harry!' I called. 'Shut up, Harry!' It was terrible, the things he was saying.

Ganderbai went out of the room as though neither of us was there and I followed him and put my arm around his shoulder as he walked across the hall and out on to the balcony.

'Don't you listen to Harry,' I said. 'This thing's made him so he doesn't know what he's saying.'

We went down the steps from the balcony to the drive and across the drive in the darkness to where his old Morris car was parked. He opened the door and got in.

'You did a wonderful job,' I said. 'Thank you so very much for coming.'

'All he needs is a good holiday,' he said quietly, without looking at me, then he started the engine and drove off.

# Skin

First published in *The New Yorker* (17 May 1952)

That year – 1946 – winter was a long time going. Although it was April, a freezing wind blew through the streets of the city, and overhead the snow clouds moved across the sky.

The old man who was called Drioli shuffled painfully along the sidewalk of the Rue de Rivoli. He was cold and miserable, huddled up like a hedgehog in a filthy black coat, only his eyes and the top of his head visible above the turned-up collar.

The door of a café opened and the faint whiff of roasting chicken brought a pain of yearning to the top of his stomach. He moved on, glancing without any interest at the things in the shop windows – perfume, silk ties and shirts, diamonds, porcelain, antique furniture, finely bound books. Then a picture gallery. He had always liked picture galleries. This one had a single canvas on display in the window. He stopped to look at it. He turned to go on. He checked, looked back; and now, suddenly, there came to him a slight uneasiness, a movement of the memory, a distant recollection of something, somewhere, he had seen before. He looked again. It was a landscape, a clump of trees leaning madly over to one side as if blown by a tremendous wind, the sky swirling and twisting all around.

Attached to the frame there was a little plaque, and on this it said: CHAÏM SOUTINE (1894–1943).

Drioli stared at the picture, wondering vaguely what there was about it that seemed familiar. Crazy painting, he thought. Very strange and crazy – but I like it . . . Chaïm Soutine . . . Soutine . . . 'By God!' he cried suddenly. 'My little Kalmuck, that's who it is! My little Kalmuck with a picture in the finest shop in Paris! Just imagine that!'

The old man pressed his face closer to the window. He could remember the boy – yes, quite clearly he could remember him. But when? When? The rest of it was not so easy to recollect. It was so long ago. How long? Twenty – no, more like thirty years, wasn't it? Wait a minute. Yes – it was the year before the war, the first war, 1913. That was it. And this Soutine, this ugly little Kalmuck, a sullen brooding boy whom he had liked – almost loved – for no reason at all that he could think of except that he could paint.

And how he could paint! It was coming back more clearly now – the street, the line of refuse cans along the length of it, the rotten smell, the brown cats walking delicately over the refuse, and then the women, moist fat women sitting on the doorsteps with their feet upon the cobblestones of the street. Which street? Where was it the boy had lived?

The Cité Falguière, that was it! The old man nodded his head several times, pleased to have remembered the name. Then there was the studio with the single chair in it, and the filthy red couch that the boy had used for sleeping; the drunken parties, the cheap white wine, the furious quarrels, and always, always the bitter sullen face of the boy brooding over his work.

It was odd, Drioli thought, how easily it all came back to him now, how each single small remembered fact seemed instantly to remind him of another.

There was that nonsense with the tattoo, for instance. Now, *that* was a mad thing if ever there was one. How had it started? Ah, yes – he had got rich one day, that was it, and he had bought lots of wine. He could see himself now as he entered the studio with the parcel of bottles under his arm – the boy sitting before the easel, and his (Drioli's) own wife standing in the centre of the room, posing for her picture.

'Tonight we shall celebrate,' he said. 'We shall have a little celebration, us three.'

'What is it that we celebrate?' the boy asked without looking up. 'Is it that you have decided to divorce your wife so she can marry me?'

'No,' Drioli said. 'We celebrate because today I have made a great sum of money with my work.'

'And I have made nothing. We can celebrate that also.'

'If you like.' Drioli was standing by the table unwrapping the parcel. He felt tired and he wanted to get at the wine. Nine clients in one day was all very nice, but it could play hell with a man's eyes. He had never done as many as nine before. Nine boozy soldiers – and the remarkable thing was that no fewer than seven of them had been able to pay in cash. This had made him extremely rich. But the work was terrible on the eyes. Drioli's eyes were half

closed from fatigue, the whites streaked with little con-
necting lines of red; and about an inch behind each eyeball
there was a small concentration of pain. But it was evening now and he was wealthy as a pig, and in the parcel
there were three bottles – one for his wife, one for his
friend and one for him. He had found the corkscrew and
was drawing the corks from the bottles, each making a
small plop as it came out.

The boy put down his brush. 'Oh Christ,' he said. 'How
can one work with all this going on?'

The girl came across the room to look at the painting.
Drioli came over also, holding a bottle in one hand, a glass
in the other.

'No!' the boy shouted, blazing up suddenly. 'Please –
no!' He snatched the canvas from the easel and stood it
against the wall. But Drioli had seen it.

'I like it.'

'It's terrible.'

'It's marvellous. Like all the others that you do, it's
marvellous. I love them all.'

'The trouble is,' the boy said, scowling, 'that in themselves they are not nourishing. I cannot eat them.'

'But still they are marvellous.' Drioli handed him a
tumblerful of the pale-yellow wine. 'Drink it,' he said. 'It
will make you happy.'

Never, he thought, had he known a more unhappy person, or one with a gloomier face. He had spotted him in a
café some seven months before, drinking alone, and
because he had looked like a Russian or some sort of an
Asiatic, Drioli had sat down at his table and talked.

'You are a Russian?'

'Yes.'

'Where from?'

'Minsk.'

Drioli had jumped up and embraced him, crying that he too had been born in that city.

'It wasn't actually Minsk,' the boy had said. 'But quite near.'

'Where?'

'Smilovichi, about twelve miles away.'

'Smilovichi!' Drioli had shouted, embracing him again. 'I walked there several times when I was a boy.' Then he had sat down again, staring affectionately at the other's face. 'You know,' he had said, 'you don't look like a western Russian. You're like a Tartar, or a Kalmuck. You look exactly like a Kalmuck.'

Now, standing in the studio, Drioli looked again at the boy as he took the glass of wine and tipped it down his throat in one swallow. Yes, he did have a face like a Kalmuck – very broad and high-cheeked, with a wide coarse nose. This broadness of the cheeks was accentuated by the ears, which stood out sharply from the head. And then he had the narrow eyes, the black hair, the thick sullen mouth of a Kalmuck; but the hands – the hands were always a surprise, so small and white like a lady's, with tiny thin fingers.

'Give me some more,' the boy said. 'If we are to celebrate, then let us do it properly.'

Drioli distributed the wine and sat himself on a chair.

The boy sat on the old couch with Drioli's wife. The three bottles were placed on the floor between them.

'Tonight we shall drink as much as we possibly can,' Drioli said. 'I am exceptionally rich. I think perhaps I should go out now and buy some more bottles. How many shall I get?'

'Six more,' the boy said. 'Two for each.'

'Good. I shall go now and fetch them.'

'And I will help you.'

In the nearest café Drioli bought six bottles of white wine, and they carried them back to the studio. They placed them on the floor in two rows, and Drioli fetched the corkscrew and pulled the corks, all six of them; then they sat down again and continued to drink.

'It is only the very wealthy,' Drioli said, 'who can afford to celebrate in this manner.'

'That is true,' the boy said. 'Isn't that true, Josie?'

'Of course.'

'How do you feel, Josie?'

'Fine.'

'Will you leave Drioli and marry me?'

'No.'

'Beautiful wine,' Drioli said. 'It is a privilege to drink it.'

Slowly, methodically, they set about getting themselves drunk. The process was routine, but all the same there was a certain ceremony to be observed, and a gravity to be maintained, and a great number of things to be said, then said again – and the wine must be praised, and the slowness was important too, so that there would be time to savour the three delicious stages of transition, especially (for Drioli) the one when he began to float and his feet did not really belong to him. That was the best period of them all – when he could look down at his feet and they were so far away that he would wonder what crazy person they might belong to and why they were lying around on the floor like that, in the distance.

After a while, he got up to switch on the light. He was surprised to see that the feet came with him when he did this, especially because he couldn't feel them touching the ground. It gave him a pleasant sensation of walking on air. Then he began wandering around the room, peeking slyly at the canvases stacked against the walls.

'Listen,' he said at length. 'I have an idea.' He came across and stood before the couch, swaying gently. 'Listen, my little Kalmuck.'

'What?'

'I have a tremendous idea. Are you listening?'

'I'm listening to Josie.'

'Listen to me, *please*. You are my friend – my ugly little Kalmuck from Minsk – and to me you are such an artist that I would like to have a picture, a lovely picture –'

'Have them all. Take all you can find, but do not interrupt me when I am talking with your wife.'

'No, no. Now listen. I mean a picture that I can have with me always . . . forever . . . wherever I go . . . whatever happens . . . but always with me . . . a picture by you.' He reached forward and shook the boy's knee. 'Now listen to me, *please*.'

'Listen to him,' the girl said.

'It is this. I want you to paint a picture on my skin, on my back. Then I want you to tattoo over what you have painted so that it will be there always.'

'You have crazy ideas.'

'I will teach you how to use the tattoo. It is easy. A child could do it.'

'I am not a child.'

'*Please . . .*'

'You are quite mad. What is it you want?' The painter looked up into the slow, dark, wine-bright eyes of the other man. 'What in heaven's name is it you want?'

'You could do it easily! You could! You could!'

'You mean with the tattoo?'

'Yes, with the tattoo! I will teach you in two minutes!'

'Impossible!'

'Are you saying I don't know what I'm talking about?'

No, the boy could not possibly be saying that because if anyone knew about the tattoo it was he – Drioli. Had he not, only last month, covered a man's whole belly with the most wonderful and delicate design composed entirely of flowers? What about the client who had had so much hair upon his chest that he had done him a picture of a grizzly bear so designed that the hair on the chest became the furry coat of the bear? Could he not draw the likeness of a lady and position it with such subtlety upon a man's arm that when the muscle of the arm was flexed the lady came to life and performed some astonishing contortions?

'All I am saying,' the boy told him, 'is that you are drunk and this is a drunken idea.'

'We could have Josie for a model. A study of Josie upon

my back. Am I not entitled to a picture of my wife upon my back?'

'Of Josie?'

'Yes.' Drioli knew he only had to mention his wife and the boy's thick brown lips would loosen and begin to quiver.

'No,' the girl said.

'Darling Josie, *please*. Take this bottle and finish it, then you will feel more generous. It is an enormous idea. Never in my life have I had such an idea before.'

'What idea?'

'That he should make a picture of you upon my back. Am I not entitled to that?'

'A picture of me?'

'A nude study,' the boy said. 'It is an agreeable idea.'

'Not nude,' the girl said.

'It is an enormous idea,' Drioli said.

'It's a damn crazy idea,' the girl said.

'It is in any event an idea,' the boy said. 'It is an idea that calls for a celebration.'

They emptied another bottle among them. Then the boy said, 'It is no good. I could not possibly manage the tattoo. Instead, I will paint this picture on your back and you will have it with you so long as you do not take a bath and wash it off. If you never take a bath again in your life then you will have it always, as long as you live.'

'No,' Drioli said.

'Yes – and on the day that you decide to take a bath I will know that you do not any longer value my picture. It will be a test of your admiration for my art.'

'I do not like the idea,' the girl said. 'His admiration for your art is so great that he would be unclean for many years. Let us have the tattoo. But not nude.'

'Then just the head,' Drioli said.

'I could not manage it.'

'It is immensely simple. I will undertake to teach you in two minutes. You will see. I shall go now and fetch the instruments. The needles and the inks. I have inks of many different colours – as many different colours as you have paints, and far more beautiful . . .'

'It is impossible.'

'I have many inks. Have I not many different colours of inks, Josie?'

'Yes.'

'You will see,' Drioli said. 'I will go now and fetch them.' He got up from his chair and walked unsteadily, but with determination, out of the room.

In half an hour Drioli was back. 'I have brought everything,' he cried, waving a brown suitcase. 'All the necessities of the tattooist are here in this bag.'

He placed the bag on the table, opened it, and laid out the electric needles and the small bottles of coloured inks. He plugged in the electric needle, then he took the instrument in his hand and pressed a switch. It made a buzzing sound and the quarter inch of needle that projected from the end of it began to vibrate swiftly up and down. He threw off his jacket and rolled up his left sleeve. 'Now look. Watch me and I will show you how easy it is. I will make a design on my arm, here.'

His forearm was already covered with blue markings,

but he selected a small clear patch of skin upon which to demonstrate.

'First, I choose my ink – let us use ordinary blue – and I dip the point of my needle in the ink . . . so . . . and I hold the needle up straight and I run it lightly over the surface of the skin . . . like this . . . and with the little motor and the electricity, the needle jumps up and down and punctures the skin and the ink goes in and there you are . . . See how easy it is . . . see how I draw a picture of a greyhound here upon my arm . . .'

The boy was intrigued. 'Now let *me* practise a little – on your arm.'

With the buzzing needle he began to draw blue lines upon Drioli's arm. 'It is simple,' he said. 'It is like drawing with pen and ink. There is no difference except that it is slower.'

'There is nothing to it. Are you ready? Shall we begin?'

'At once.'

'The model!' cried Drioli. 'Come on, Josie!' He was in a bustle of enthusiasm now, tottering around the room arranging everything, like a child preparing for some exciting game. 'Where will you have her? Where shall she stand?'

'Let her be standing there, by my dressing-table. Let her be brushing her hair. I will paint her with her hair down over her shoulders and her brushing it.'

'Tremendous. You are a genius.'

Reluctantly, the girl walked over and stood by the dressing-table, carrying her glass of wine with her.

Drioli pulled off his shirt and stepped out of his trousers. He retained only his underpants and his socks and shoes, and he stood there, swaying gently from side to side, his small body firm, white-skinned, almost hairless. 'Now,' he said, 'I am the canvas. Where will you place your canvas?'

'As always, upon the easel.'

'Don't be crazy. I am the canvas.'

'Then place yourself upon the easel. That is where you belong.'

'How can I?'

'Are you the canvas or are you not the canvas?'

'I am the canvas. Already I begin to feel like a canvas.'

'Then place yourself upon the easel. There should be no difficulty.'

'Truly, it is not possible.'

'Then sit on the chair. Sit back to front, then you can lean your drunken head against the back of it. Hurry now, for I am about to commence.'

'I am ready. I am waiting.'

'First,' the boy said, 'I shall make an ordinary painting. Then, if it pleases me, I shall tattoo over it.' With a wide brush he began to paint upon the naked skin of the man's back.

'Ayee! Ayee!' Drioli screamed. 'A monstrous centipede is marching down my spine!'

'Be still now! Be still!' The boy worked rapidly, applying the paint only in a thin blue wash so that it would not afterwards interfere with the process of tattooing. His concentration, as soon as he began to paint, was so great that it appeared somehow to supersede his drunkenness. He applied the brush strokes with quick short jabs of the arm, holding the wrist stiff, and in less than half an hour it was finished.

'All right. That's all,' he said to the girl, who immediately returned to the couch, lay down and fell asleep.

Drioli remained awake. He watched the boy take up the needle and dip it in the ink; then he felt the sharp tickling sting as it touched the skin of his back. The pain, which was unpleasant but never extreme, kept him from going to sleep. By following the track of the needle and by watching the different colours of ink that the boy was using, Drioli amused himself trying to visualize what was going on behind him. The boy worked with an astonishing intensity. He appeared to have become completely absorbed in the little machine and in the unusual effects it was able to produce.

Far into the small hours of the morning the machine buzzed and the boy worked. Drioli could remember that when the artist finally stepped back and said, 'It is finished,' there was daylight outside and the sound of people walking in the street.

'I want to see it,' Drioli said. The boy held up a mirror, at an angle, and Drioli craned his neck to look.

'Good God!' he cried. It was a startling sight. The whole of his back, from the top of the shoulders to the base of the spine, was a blaze of colour – gold and green and blue and black and scarlet. The tattoo was applied so heavily it looked almost like an impasto. The boy had followed as closely as possible the original brush strokes, filling them in solid, and it was marvellous the way he had made use of the spine and the protrusion of the shoulder blades so that they became part of the composition. What is more, he had somehow managed to achieve – even with this slow process – a certain spontaneity. The portrait was quite alive; it contained much of that twisted, tortured quality so characteristic of Soutine's other work. It was not a good likeness. It was a mood rather than a likeness, the model's face vague and tipsy, the background swirling around her head in a mass of dark-green curling strokes.

'It's tremendous!'

'I rather like it myself.' The boy stood back, examining it critically. 'You know,' he added, 'I think it's good enough for me to sign.' And taking up the buzzer again, he inscribed his name in red ink on the right-hand side, over the place where Drioli's kidney was.

The old man who was called Drioli was standing in a sort of trance, staring at the painting in the window of the picture-dealer's shop. It had been so long ago, all that – almost as though it had happened in another life.

And the boy? What had become of him? He could remember now that after returning from the war – the first war – he had missed him and had questioned Josie.

'Where is my little Kalmuck?'

'He is gone,' she had answered. 'I do not know where, but I heard it said that a dealer had taken him up and sent him away to Céret to make more paintings.'

'Perhaps he will return.'

'Perhaps he will. Who knows?'

That was the last time they had mentioned him. Shortly afterwards they had moved to Le Havre, where there were more sailors and business was better. The old man smiled as he remembered Le Havre. Those were the pleasant years, the years between the wars, with the small shop near the docks and the comfortable rooms and always enough work, with every day three, four, five sailors coming and wanting pictures on their arms. Those were truly the pleasant years.

Then had come the second war, and Josie being killed, and the Germans arriving, and that was the finish of his business. No one had wanted pictures on their arms any more after that. And by that time he was too old for any other kind of work. In desperation he had made his way back to Paris, hoping vaguely that things would be easier in the big city. But they were not.

And now, after the war was over, he possessed neither the means nor the energy to start up his small business again. It wasn't very easy for an old man to know what to do, especially when one did not like to beg. Yet how else could he keep alive?

Well, he thought, still staring at the picture. So that is my little Kalmuck. And how quickly the sight of one small object such as this can stir the memory. Up to a few moments ago he had even forgotten that he had a tattoo on his back. It had been ages since he had thought about it. He put his face closer to the window and looked into the gallery. On the walls he could see many other pictures and all seemed to be the work of the same artist. There were a great number of people strolling around. Obviously it was a special exhibition.

On a sudden impulse, Drioli turned, pushed open the door of the gallery and went in.

It was a long room with a thick wine-coloured carpet, and by God how beautiful and warm it was! There were all these people strolling about looking at the pictures, well-washed, dignified people, each of whom held a catalogue in the hand. Drioli stood just inside the door, nervously glancing around, wondering whether he dared go forward and mingle with this crowd. But before he had had time to gather his courage, he heard a voice beside him saying, 'What is it you want?'

The speaker wore a black morning coat. He was plump and short and had a very white face. It was a flabby face with so much flesh upon it that the cheeks hung down on either side of the mouth in two fleshy collops, spaniel-wise. He came up close to Drioli and said again, 'What is it you want?'

Drioli stood still.

'If you please,' the man was saying, 'take yourself out of my gallery.'

'Am I not permitted to look at the pictures?'

'I have asked you to leave.'

Drioli stood his ground. He felt suddenly, overwhelmingly outraged.

'Let us not have trouble,' the man was saying. 'Come on now, this way.' He put a fat white paw on Drioli's arm and began to push him firmly to the door.

That did it. 'Take your goddam hands off me!' Drioli shouted. His voice rang clear down the long gallery and all the heads jerked around as one – all the startled faces stared down the length of the room at the person who had made this noise. A flunkey came running over to help, and the two men tried to hustle Drioli through the door. The people stood still, watching the struggle. Their faces expressed only a mild interest, and seemed to be saying, 'It's all right. There's no danger to us. It's being taken care of.'

'I, too!' Drioli was shouting. 'I, too, have a picture by this painter! He was my friend and I have a picture which he gave me!'

'He's mad.'

'A lunatic. A raving lunatic.'

'Someone should call the police.'

With a rapid twist of the body Drioli suddenly jumped clear of the two men, and before anyone could stop him he was running down the gallery shouting. 'I'll show you! I'll show you! I'll show you!' He flung off his overcoat, then his jacket and shirt, and he turned so that his naked back was towards the people.

'There!' he cried, breathing quickly. 'You see? There it is!'

There was a sudden absolute silence in the room, each person arrested in what he was doing, standing motionless in a kind of shocked, uneasy bewilderment. They were staring at the tattooed picture. It was still there, the colours as bright as ever, but the old man's back was thinner now, the shoulder blades protruded more sharply, and the effect, though not great, was to give the picture a curiously wrinkled, squashed appearance.

Somebody said, 'My God, but it is!'

Then came the excitement and the noise of voices as the people surged forward to crowd round the old man.

'It is unmistakable!'

'His early manner, yes?'

'It is fantastic, fantastic!'

'And look, it is signed!'

'Bend your shoulders forward, my friend, so that the picture stretches out flat.'

'Old one, when was this done?'

'In 1913,' Drioli said, without turning around. 'In the autumn of 1913.'

'Who taught Soutine to tattoo?'

'I taught him.'

'And the woman?'

'She was my wife.'

The gallery owner was pushing through the crowd towards Drioli. He was calm now, deadly serious, making a smile with his mouth. 'Monsieur,' he said, 'I will buy it.' Drioli could see the loose fat upon the face vibrating as he moved his jaw. 'I said I will buy it, Monsieur.'

'How can you buy it?' Drioli asked softly.

'I will give two hundred thousand francs for it.' The dealer's eyes were small and dark, the wings of his broad nose-base were beginning to quiver.

'Don't do it!' someone murmured in the crowd. 'It is worth twenty times as much.'

Drioli opened his mouth to speak. No words came, so he shut it; then he opened it again and said slowly, 'But how can I sell it?' He lifted his hands, let them drop loosely to his sides. 'Monsieur, how can I possibly sell it?' All the sadness in the world was in his voice.

'Yes!' they were saying in the crowd. 'How can he sell it? It is a part of himself!'

'Listen,' the dealer said, coming up close. 'I will help

you. I will make you rich. Together we shall make some private arrangement over this picture, no?'

Drioli watched him with slow, apprehensive eyes. 'But how can you buy it, Monsieur? What will you do with it when you have bought it? Where will you keep it? Where will you keep it tonight? And where tomorrow?'

'Ah, where will I keep it? Yes, where will I keep it? Now, where will I keep it? Well, now . . .' The dealer stroked the bridge of his nose with a fat white finger. 'It would seem,' he said, 'that if I take the picture, I take you also. That is a disadvantage.' He paused and stroked his nose again. 'The picture itself is of no value until you are dead. How old are you, my friend?'

'Sixty-one.'

'But you are perhaps not very robust, no?' The dealer lowered the hand from his nose and looked Drioli up and down, slowly, like a farmer appraising an old horse.

'I do not like this,' Drioli said, edging away. 'Quite honestly, Monsieur, I do not like it.' He edged straight into the arms of a tall man, who put out his hands and caught him gently by the shoulders. Drioli glanced around and apologized. The man smiled down at him, patting one of the old fellow's naked shoulders reassuringly with a hand encased in a canary-coloured glove.

'Listen, my friend,' the stranger said, still smiling. 'Do you like to swim and bask yourself in the sun?'

Drioli looked up at him, rather startled.

'Do you like fine food and red wine from the great châteaux of Bordeaux?' The man was still smiling, showing strong white teeth with a flash of gold among them. He spoke in a soft coaxing manner, one gloved hand still resting on Drioli's shoulder. 'Do you like such things?'

'Well – yes,' Drioli answered, still greatly perplexed. 'Of course.'

'And the company of beautiful women?'

'Why not?'

'And a cupboard full of suits and shirts made to your own personal measurements? It would seem that you are a little lacking for clothes.'

Drioli watched this suave man, waiting for the rest of the proposition.

'Have you ever had a shoe constructed especially for your own foot?'

'No.'

'You would like that?'

'Well . . .'

'And a man who will shave you in the mornings and trim your hair?'

Drioli simply stood and gaped.

'And a plump attractive girl to manicure the nails of your fingers?'

Someone in the crowd giggled.

'And a bell beside your bed to summon a maid to bring your breakfast in the morning? Would you like these things, my friend? Do they appeal to you?'

Drioli stood still and looked at him.

'You see, I am the owner of the Hotel Bristol in Cannes. I now invite you to come down there and live as my guest for the rest of your life in luxury and comfort.' The man paused, allowing his listener time to savour this cheerful prospect.

'Your only duty – shall I call it your pleasure – will be to spend your time on my beach in bathing trunks, walking among my guests, sunning yourself, swimming, drinking cocktails. You would like that?'

There was no answer.

'Don't you see – all the guests will thus be able to observe this fascinating picture by Soutine. You will become famous, and men will say, "Look, there is the fellow with ten million francs upon his back." You like this idea, Monsieur? It pleases you?'

Drioli looked up at the tall man in the canary gloves, still wondering whether this was some sort of a joke. 'It is a comical idea,' he said slowly. 'But do you really mean it?'

'Of course I mean it.'

'Wait,' the dealer interrupted. 'See here, old one. Here is the answer to our problem. I will buy the picture, and I will arrange with a surgeon to remove the skin from your back, and then you will be able to go off on your own and enjoy the great sum of money I shall give you for it.'

'With no skin on my back?'

'No, no, please! You misunderstand. This surgeon will put a new piece of skin in the place of the old one. It is simple.'

'Could he do that?'

'There is nothing to it.'

'Impossible!' said the man with the canary gloves. 'He's too old for such a major skin-grafting operation. It would kill him. It would kill you, my friend.'

'It would kill me?'

'Naturally. You would never survive. Only the picture would come through.'

'In the name of God!' Drioli cried. He looked around aghast at the faces of the people watching him, and in the silence that followed, another man's voice, speaking quietly from the back of the group, could be heard saying, 'Perhaps, if one were to offer this old man enough money, he might consent to kill himself on the spot. Who knows?' A few people sniggered. The dealer moved his feet uneasily on the carpet.

Then the hand in the canary glove was tapping Drioli again upon the shoulder. 'Come on,' the man was saying, smiling his broad white smile. 'You and I will go and have a good dinner and we can talk about it some more while we eat. How's that? Are you hungry?'

Drioli watched him, frowning. He didn't like the man's long flexible neck, or the way he craned it forward at you when he spoke, like a snake.

'Roast duck and Chambertin,' the man was saying. He put a rich succulent accent on the words, splashing them out with his tongue. 'And perhaps a *soufflé aux marrons*, light and frothy.'

Drioli's eyes turned up towards the ceiling, his lips became loose and wet. One could see the poor old fellow beginning literally to drool at the mouth.

'How do you like your duck?' the man went on. 'Do you like it very brown and crisp outside, or shall it be . . .'

'I am coming,' Drioli said quickly. Already he had picked up his shirt and was pulling it frantically over his head. 'Wait for me, Monsieur. I am coming.' And within a minute he had disappeared out of the gallery with his new patron.

It wasn't more than a few weeks later that a picture by Soutine, of a woman's head, painted in an unusual manner, nicely framed and heavily varnished, turned up for sale in Buenos Aires. That – and the fact that there is no hotel in Cannes called Bristol – causes one to wonder a little, and to pray for the old man's health, and to hope fervently that wherever he may be at this moment, there is a plump attractive girl to manicure the nails of his fingers, and a maid to bring him his breakfast in bed in the mornings.

# The Princess and the Poacher

First published in *Two Fables* (1986)

Although Hengist was now eighteen years old, he still showed no desire to follow in his father's trade of basket-weaving. He even refused to go out and collect the osiers from the riverbank. This saddened his parents greatly, but they were wise enough to know that it seldom pays to force a young lad to work at something when his heart is not in it.

In appearance, Hengist was an exceedingly unattractive youth. With his squat body, his short bandy legs, his extra-long arms and his crumpled face, he looked almost as though there might be a touch of the ape or the gorilla about him. He was certainly mighty strong. He could bend double a two-inch-thick iron bar with his hands alone, and once he had astonished an old carter whose horse had fallen into a ditch by lifting the animal out bodily in his arms and placing it back on the road.

Quite naturally, Hengist was interested in maidens fair. But as one might expect, no maidens, fair or otherwise, were interested in Hengist. He was a pleasant enough fel-low, there was no doubt about that, but there is a limit to the degree of ugliness any woman can tolerate in a man. Hengist was well beyond that limit. In fact, his ugliness was so extreme that no female other than his mother would have anything to do with him. This was a great sorrow to the lad. It was also grossly unfair, because no man is responsible for his own looks.

Poor Hengist. Although he knew that every maid and every wench in the Kingdom was far beyond his reach for ever, he continued to long for them and lust after them with unabated passion. Whenever he spied a girl milking a cow or hanging out the washing, he would stop and stare and yearn most terribly to possess her.

Fortunately for him, he was soon to find another outlet for his energies. It had become a habit of his to take long walks in the countryside, through the forests and the glens, to cool his ardour, and over the ensuing weeks he began in some subtle way to fall in love with the landscape of the open air. He would spend his days roaming in deserted places, a silent, solitary, terribly uncouth figure, communing with nature. And thus, gradually and inevitably, he came to learn a great deal about the habits of animals and birds. He also discovered to his delight that he possessed the ability to move so silently through the forest that he could come within arm's length of a timid creature like a hare or a deer before it was aware of his presence. This was not just from practice. It appeared to be a gift that had been bestowed upon him, a rare ability to merge into the landscape and suddenly to emerge again, almost like a ghost, when no man or bird or beast had seen him coming.

His family were very poor and they hardly ever tasted meat or game from one year to the next. Quite understandably, and quite soon, it dawned upon Hengist that he could very easily improve their lot, and indeed his own, by

doing a little poaching. He be
partridge once a week, but it w.
pleasure and excitement of the
Here, after all, was something he
well. Poaching was an art. The thri
crouching hare undetected or of si
pheasant from a branch gave him a sen
such as he had never known before. He                 ucted
to the sport.

But poaching was a hazardous occupation in the Kingdom. All the land, all the forests and the streams, were
owned either by the King himself or by one of the great
Dukes, and although the footpaths on their estates were
open to the public for strolling quietly, poaching on these
lands was strictly forbidden. Anyone who strayed off the
designated footpaths did so at his peril. The undergrowth
was strewn with cunningly concealed man-traps whose
iron jaws could bite a man's leg to the bone if he stepped
on the plate that released the spring. And there the poor
captive would remain, pinned to the ground, until a patrol-
ling keeper found him the next day.

In the eyes of the King and the Dukes, poaching was a
greater crime than murder. The sentence for murder was
simply death by hanging, but the sentence for poaching
was far more unpleasant. A convicted poacher would first
be weighed on a special balance. Then two leaden anklets
would be constructed whose weight had been most carefully calculated by the Royal Mathematician. These anklets
would be fastened around the victim's ankles and his
hands tied behind his back before he was lowered into the

Tub that was built of stone and stood
in the Market Square of the capital. The
height had also been measured beforehand by the
Mathematician, and a quantity of water had either been
added to or taken out of the Tub so that when the man
stood on tiptoe on the bottom, the top of his head was
just below the surface of the water. The result of all this
was that the victim spent many hours, sometimes days,
being pulled down by the weight of the anklets, then
jumping up again for a quick breath of air when his feet
touched the bottom. Finally he sank altogether from
exhaustion. The uncomfortable nature of this punish-
ment did much to discourage the population from
breaking the law of the land. The hunting of game was
the prerogative only of the Royal Family and the Dukes.

But Hengist was not to be intimidated. He had such
faith in his powers of stealth that he harboured no fears
of the dreaded Drowning Tub. His parents were, of
course, frightened out of their skins. Every evening when
he went out, and every dawn when he returned with a
juicy partridge or a leveret under his coat, they trembled
for their son, and indeed for themselves. But hunger is a
powerful persuader and the spoils were always accepted
and roasted and devoured with relish.

'You *are* being careful, son, are you not?' the mother
would say, as she munched upon the tender breast of a
woodcock.

'I is always careful, ma,' Hengist would answer. 'That
little ole King and them fancy Dooks they ain't never
goin' to lay a finger on me.'

Hengist soon became so confident in his powers of poaching that he scorned the cover of darkness and took to going out in full daylight, which was something that only the bravest or the most foolhardy would do. And then one day, on a fine morning in springtime, he decided to have a go at the most protected area in the entire Kingdom, that part of the Royal Forest which lies immediately beneath the walls of the Castle itself, where the King lived. Here the game was more plentiful than anywhere else, but the dangers were tremendous. Hengist, as he crept soft and silent into the Royal Forest, was relishing this danger.

And now he was standing immobile in the shadow of a mighty beech, watching a young roebuck grazing not five paces away and waiting for the moment to pounce. Out of the edge of one eye he could see the south wall of the Royal Castle itself and somewhere in the distance he could hear bugles blowing. They were probably changing the guard at the gates, he told himself. Then suddenly, out of that same eye, he caught sight of a figure among the trees, not forty paces distant. Slowly, he turned his head to examine this person more carefully and, lo and behold, he saw immediately that it was none other than the young Princess, the only child of the King and the jewel in his crown. She was a young damsel of breathtaking beauty, with skin as pure and smooth as a silken glove, and she was but seventeen years old. Here she was then, apparently idling away the morning picking bluebells in the wood. Hengist's heart gave a jump when he saw her and all the old passions came flooding back once again. For a mad moment or two, he considered surprising the damsel by kneeling before her with whispered words of love and adoration, but he knew only too well what would happen then. She would take one look at his terrible ugliness and run away screaming, and he would be caught and put to death. It also occurred to him that he might creep upon her stealthily, coming up behind her unseen then clapping a hand over her mouth and having his way with her by force. But he quickly pushed this foul notion out of his mind, for he abhorred violence of any kind.

What happened next came very suddenly. There was a fanfare of hunting horns nearby and Hengist turned and saw a massive wild boar, the largest he had ever seen, come charging through the trees, and behind it, some fifty paces back, was riding the King himself and a group of noblemen, all galloping full-tilt after the boar with lances drawn. The Princess was right in the path of the running boar and the boar was in no mood to swerve around her. Just the opposite. An angry hunted boar will attack any human who stands in its line of flight. Worse still, it will often swing aside and attack an innocent bystander who might happen to be near. And now the boar had spotted the Princess, and it was making straight for her. Hengist saw the maiden drop her bunch of bluebells and run. Then she seemed to realize the futility of this, and she stopped and pressed herself against the trunk of a giant oak, and there she stood, helpless, with arms outspread as though for crucifixion, waiting for the madly rushing beast to reach her. Hengist saw the boar, the size of a small bull, charging forwards with head down, the two sharp, glistening tusks pointing straight at the victim.

He took off like an arrow. He flew over the ground with his feet hardly touching the earth, and when he realized that the boar was going to reach the Princess before him, he made a last, despairing dive through the air and reached far out with his hands and just managed to grab hold of the boar's tusks when they were within a fraction of the maiden's midriff. Both Hengist and the boar went tumbling over in a heap, but the youth held on to the tusks, and when he leaped to his feet again, the boar came with him, lifted on high by the strongest pair of arms in the Kingdom. Hengist gave a sudden twist with his hands and even the King, some thirty paces distant, heard the boar's cervical spine snap in two. Hengist then swung the massive beast back and forth a couple of times before sending it sailing over his head as easily as if it had been a stick of firewood.

The King reached them first, galloping like mad and reining in his frothing horse right beside his daughter. He was followed by half a dozen noblemen, who all pulled up behind the King. The King leaped from his charger crying out, 'My darling! My little child! Are you all right?' He had witnessed the whole of the four-second drama, and in truth, when he had seen the boar charging straight for his daughter, he thought she was finished. And then he had seen this extraordinary human arrow leaping and flying between the trees and flinging himself upon the terrible boar just in the nick of time. The King was white in the face as he took the sobbing Princess in his arms to

console her. Hengist stood awkwardly by, not quite knowing what to do with his hands or his feet or anything else.

At last the King turned to look at Hengist. For a
moment or two, the shock of seeing such a spectacularly
ugly youth rendered him speechless. But he kept on looking, and as he looked, he found himself liking more and
more what he saw. A man is seldom repelled by the mal-
formed features of another man. Quite the reverse. Men,
as a whole, take less kindly to other men who are exceptionally good-looking. Women are often the same with
other women. Yet, as we all know, good looks do have a
profound influence upon the *opposite* sex. This is a fact of
life, but as the wise King knew, it caused much disillusionment later on. Yes, the King was telling himself, as he
continued to stare at this curious fellow who stood before
him, how different he is from the sloppy, effeminate, lecherous young courtiers who surround me at the Castle!
This is a real man! He is brave and swift and fearless, and
to hell with his looks! It was at this point that a sly plot
began to hatch in the King's devious mind.

In his rich royal voice, charged with emotion, he said,
'Young man, today you have done me the greatest service
any citizen could perform for his King! You have saved
the treasure of my life, the pearl of my Kingdom, my only
child, indeed the only child I shall ever have because the
poor Queen is dead! I intend to see that you are rewarded
in a munificent manner! Pray accompany me to the Castle
at once!'

Then the King lifted the Princess up on to his charger
and himself got into the saddle behind her. The entourage

rode off at a trot, with a rather bemused Hengist running alongside.

As soon as he arrived at the Castle, the King summoned a meeting of the Elders. Ostensibly, these old men were the parliament that ruled the Kingdom, but in reality it was the King himself who decided everything. No man dared gainsay the monarch.

In the Council Chamber the Elders, twenty in all, were assembled in their pews.

Above, on a dais, sat the King upon his throne, and beside him stood Hengist. The latter was not very suitably attired for the occasion. He wore a shirt made from some kind of sacking, his breeches were filthy, and on his stockingless feet was a pair of home-made sandals. The Elders stared at this ugly, ill-dressed creature with distaste. The King smiled. He was a curious man, the King, much given to eccentricities and japes and ingenious practical jokes. For example, at his dining-table, which seated twelve guests, he had twelve little taps concealed under the edge of the table, and if any of his guests, male or female, annoyed him or said something foolish, the King would reach under the table and open the appropriate tap. This would send a powerful jet of water from a tiny hole in the centre of the chair right up the backside of the offending guest.

It had not taken the King long to realize that Hengist, with those terribly ugly features, must be the most sexually disappointed man in the Kingdom. He had actually observed several ladies of the court recoiling and covering their faces as the youth passed by. All this suited his subtle plan very well.

'Learned Elders,' he said, addressing the Council, 'this gallant youth, Hengist by name, has by an act of unbelievable bravery saved the life of the Princess, your future Queen. No reward is too great for him. He shall therefore be granted a stipend of one thousand gold crowns a year and shall be accommodated in a grace-and-favour mansion on the Royal Estate. He shall be provided with servants and a lavish wardrobe and whatever else he desires for his comfort.'

'Hear hear,' the Elders murmured. 'He well deserves it.'

'But that is a mere nothing compared to what other favours I am now about to grant him,' the King went on. 'I have decided that the greatest reward I can bestow upon this valiant and gallant youth is as follows. By Royal Decree, he shall also be granted . . .' Here the King paused dramatically. The Elders waited. 'He shall be granted the absolute right to ravish any maiden, wench, lady, dame, countess, duchess or other female in the Kingdom whenever he so desires.'

There was uproar among the Elders. 'You can't do that!' they cried. 'What about our wives? What about our daughters?'

'What about them?' the King asked. 'You will notice that I have not even excluded the Princess, so why should I exclude your wretched wives or daughters?'

'You mustn't do this, Your Majesty!' the Elders cried out. 'There will be chaos at court! There will be rape in the corridors! The whole place will be bedlam! Our poor innocent daughters! Our dear wives!'

'I doubt your daughters or wives will qualify,' the King remarked drily. 'Only great beauties will stand a chance of being noticed. When a man has his pick, he chooses carefully.'

'We beg you, Majesty!' the Elders cried. 'Do not force us to pass such a law!'

'Nothing you say will deter me,' said the King. 'And, furthermore, I decree that any lady who refuses to submit to the blandishments of Count Hengist – I have just made him a count, by the way – will be put to death in the Drowning Tub.'

The Elders were all on their feet waving their order papers and shouting against the King. 'You've gone too far!' they cried. 'There will be sexual anarchy in the land!'

'Don't be so sure,' said the clever King.

'Sexual anarchy!' the Elders chanted. 'Rape on the ramparts! It's not good enough!'

'Listen,' said the King, beginning to lose patience. 'I'll have the whole lot of you put in the Drowning Tub if you give me any more trouble!'

That shut them up.

'Lastly,' the King continued, 'and you'd better note this carefully, any man, any father or husband or brother, who attempts to interfere with the noble Count in the pursuance of his desires shall also be put in the Drowning Tub. Do I make myself clear?' There was a steely edge to the King's voice, and the Elders sat down and remained silent and sulked. They knew that their ruler, who had the entire army behind him to a man, was all-powerful. He always got his way.

'Draw up the Proclamation immediately,' the King said. 'Have it posted in towns and villages all over the

Kingdom. Have the town-criers call out the news in every hamlet! Tell the population that Count Hengist enjoys the freedom of all the women in the realm. And be sure to stress the penalties for disobedience. See also that Count Hengist himself be given a Card of Authority that he can wave in the face of any maiden or wench he may desire.'

Thus, this extraordinary Decree was made law, and Hengist, under the full protection of the King, moved into a mansion near the Castle where servants bathed him and groomed him and taught him how to dress in the style of the court.

At first, the poor fellow was totally bewildered. He wandered awkwardly about the Court, shunned by everybody. The Dukes snubbed him or ignored him. The ladies ran for their lives whenever he hove in sight. And who could blame them? Not even the most lascivious courtesans wanted to go near the poor fellow. He was treated by one and all as though he had leprosy.

But a strange thing had happened to Hengist. His desires seemed suddenly to have evaporated. He knew all about the immense powers he possessed. He was aware that he had the full backing of the King. He could seek out and ravish any maiden he desired, not only at court, but in the towns and villages all over the country. The trouble was, he did not desire them. He felt no urge at all. It was the old story of the forbidden fruit. Make it easy to get and the appetite goes away.

The King, who had been watching all this for several weeks with wry amusement, was strolling one morning on the ramparts with the Princess when suddenly Hengist happened by. 'How goes it, my lad?' said the King, slapping the youth on the back.

'Your Majesty,' Hengist said, 'to tell the truth, I doesn't much care for this thing you 'as done to me.'

'My dear chap,' said the King, 'what on earth is the trouble?'

'Nobody likes me around 'ere,' Hengist said. 'They is all treatin' me like dirt.'

'*I* like you,' said the Princess suddenly.

Hengist stared at her. 'You does?' he said.

'You are the only man in the Castle who does not chase me along the corridors,' the Princess said. 'You are the only decent person in the whole place.'

'Now I come to think of it, my darling,' said the King, smiling a little, 'I suppose you're right.'

'I know I'm right, Daddy,' the young beauty said. 'All the other men around here are totally disgusting. I hate them.'

'Some of them are very handsome, my dear,' the King said.

'That's got nothing to do with it!' cried the Princess. 'I don't give a fig about looks!'

'You mean you likes me a little bit?' Hengist inquired nervously.

'*Like you?*' cried the Princess, flinging herself into his arms. 'I love you!'

The King slipped away, leaving them alone. He was well pleased with the way things had worked out.

# Genesis and Catastrophe

## *A True Story*

First published as 'A Fine Son' in *Playboy*
(December 1959)

'Everything is normal,' the doctor was saying. 'Just lie back and relax.' His voice was miles away in the distance and he seemed to be shouting at her.

'You have a son.'

'What?'

'You have a fine son. You understand that, don't you? A fine son. Did you hear him crying?'

'Is he all right, Doctor?'

'Of course he is all right.'

'Please let me see him.'

'You'll see him in a moment.'

'You are certain he is all right?'

'I am quite certain.'

'Is he still crying?'

'Try to rest. There is nothing to worry about.'

'Why has he stopped crying, Doctor? What happened?'

'Don't excite yourself, please. Everything is normal.'

'I want to see him. Please let me see him.'

'Dear lady,' the doctor said, patting her hand. 'You have a fine strong healthy child. Don't you believe me when I tell you that?'

'What is the woman over there doing to him?'

'Your baby is being made to look pretty for you,' the doctor said. 'We are giving him a little wash, that is all. You must spare us a moment or two for that.'

'You swear he is all right?'

'I swear it. Now lie back and relax. Close your eyes. Go on, close your eyes. That's right. That's better. Good girl . . .'

'I have prayed and prayed that he will live, Doctor.'

'Of course he will live. What are you talking about?'

'The others didn't.'

'What?'

'None of my other ones lived, Doctor.'

The doctor stood beside the bed looking down at the pale exhausted face of the young woman. He had never seen her before today. She and her husband were new people in the town. The innkeeper's wife, who had come up to assist in the delivery, had told him that the husband worked at the local customs-house on the border and that the two of them had arrived quite suddenly at the inn with one trunk and one suitcase about three months ago. The husband was a drunkard, the innkeeper's wife had said, an arrogant, overbearing, bullying little drunkard, but the young woman was gentle and religious. And she was very sad. She never smiled. In the few weeks that she had been here, the innkeeper's wife had never once seen her smile. Also there was a rumour that this was the husband's third marriage, that one wife had died and that the other had divorced him for unsavoury reasons. But that was only a rumour.

The doctor bent down and pulled the sheet up a little

higher over the patient's chest. 'You have nothing to worry about,' he said gently. 'This is a perfectly normal baby.'

'That's exactly what they told me about the others. But I lost them all, Doctor. In the last eighteen months I have lost all three of my children, so you mustn't blame me for being anxious.'

'Three?'

'This is my fourth . . . in four years.'

The doctor shifted his feet uneasily on the bare floor.

'I don't think you know what it means, Doctor, to lose them all, all three of them, slowly, separately, one by one. I keep seeing them. I can see Gustav's face now as clearly as if he were lying here beside me in the bed. Gustav was a lovely boy, Doctor. But he was always ill. It is terrible when they are always ill and there is nothing you can do to help them.'

'I know.'

The woman opened her eyes, stared up at the doctor for a few seconds, then closed them again.

'My little girl was called Ida. She died a few days before Christmas. That is only four months ago. I just wish you could have seen Ida, Doctor.'

'You have a new one now.'

'But Ida was so beautiful.'

'Yes,' the doctor said. 'I know.'

'How can you know?' she cried.

'I am sure that she was a lovely child. But this new one is also like that.' The doctor turned away from the bed and walked over to the window and stood there looking out. It was a wet grey April afternoon, and across the street he could see the red roofs of the houses and the huge rain-drops splashing on the tiles.

'Ida was two years old, Doctor . . . and she was so beautiful I was never able to take my eyes off her from the time I dressed her in the morning until she was safe in bed again at night. I used to live in holy terror of something happening to that child. Gustav had gone and my little Otto had also gone and she was all I had left. Sometimes I used to get up in the night and creep over to the cradle and put my ear close to her mouth just to make sure that she was breathing.'

'Try to rest,' the doctor said, going back to the bed. 'Please try to rest.' The woman's face was white and blood-less, and there was a slight bluish-grey tinge around the nostrils and the mouth. A few strands of damp hair hung down over her forehead, sticking to the skin.

'When she died . . . I was already pregnant again when that happened, Doctor. This new one was a good four months on its way when Ida died. "I don't want it!" I shouted after the funeral. "I won't have it! I have buried enough children!" And my husband . . . he was strolling among the guests with a big glass of beer in his hand . . . he turned around quickly and said, "I have news for you, Klara, I have good news." Can you imagine that, Doctor? We have just buried our third child and he stands there with a glass of beer in his hand and tells me that he has good news. "Today I have been posted to Braunau," he says, "so you can start packing at once. This will be a new start for you, Klara," he says. "It will be a new place and you can have a new doctor . . ."'

'Please don't talk any more.'

'You *are* the new doctor, aren't you, Doctor?'

'That's right.'

'And here we are in Braunau.'

'Yes.'

'I am frightened, Doctor.'

'Try not to be frightened.'

'What chance can the fourth one have now?'

'You must stop thinking like that.'

'I can't help it. I am certain there is something inherited that causes my children to die in this way. There must be.'

'That is nonsense.'

'Do you know what my husband said to me when Otto was born, Doctor? He came into the room and he looked into the cradle where Otto was lying and he said, "Why do *all* my children have to be so small and weak?"'

'I am sure he didn't say that.'

'He put his head right into Otto's cradle as though he were examining a tiny insect and he said, "All I am saying is why can't they be better *specimens*? That's all I am saying." And three days after that, Otto was dead. We baptized him quickly on the third day and he died the same evening. And then Gustav died. And then Ida died. All of them died, Doctor . . . and suddenly the whole house was empty . . .'

'Don't think about it now.'

'Is this one so very small?'

'He is a normal child.'

'But small?'

'He is a little small, perhaps. But the small ones are

often a lot tougher than the big ones. Just imagine, Frau Hitler, this time next year he will be almost learning how to walk. Isn't that a lovely thought?'

She didn't answer this.

'And two years from now he will probably be talking his head off and driving you crazy with his chatter. Have you settled on a name for him yet?'

'A name?'

'Yes.'

'I don't know. I'm not sure. I think my husband said that if it was a boy we were going to call him Adolfus.'

'That means he would be called Adolf.'

'Yes. My husband likes Adolf because it has a certain similarity to Alois. My husband is called Alois.'

'Excellent.'

'Oh no!' she cried, starting up suddenly from the pillow. 'That's the same question they asked me when Otto was born! It means he is going to die! You are going to baptize him at once!'

'Now, now,' the doctor said, taking her gently by the shoulders. 'You are quite wrong. I promise you you are wrong. I was simply being an inquisitive old man, that is all. I love talking about names. I think Adolfus is a particularly fine name. It is one of my favourites. And look – here he comes now.'

The innkeeper's wife, carrying the baby high up on her enormous bosom, came sailing across the room towards the bed. 'Here is the little beauty!' she cried, beaming. 'Would you like to hold him, my dear? Shall I put him beside you?'

'Is he well wrapped?' the doctor asked. 'It is extremely cold in here.'

'Certainly he is well wrapped.'

The baby was tightly swaddled in a white woollen shawl, and only the tiny pink head protruded. The inn-keeper's wife placed him gently on the bed beside the mother. 'There you are,' she said. 'Now you can lie there and look at him to your heart's content.'

'I think you will like him,' the doctor said, smiling. 'He is a fine little baby.'

'He has the most lovely hands!' the innkeeper's wife claimed. 'Such long delicate fingers!'

The mother didn't move. She didn't even turn her head to look.

'Go on!' cried the innkeeper's wife. 'He won't bite you!'

'I am frightened to look. I don't dare to believe that I have another baby and that he is all right.'

'Don't be so stupid.'

Slowly, the mother turned her head and looked at the small, incredibly serene face that lay on the pillow beside her.

'Is this my baby?'

'Of course.'

'Oh . . . oh . . . but he is beautiful.'

The doctor turned away and went over to the table and began putting his things into his bag. The mother lay on the bed gazing at the child and smiling and touching him and making little noises of pleasure. 'Hello, Adolfus,' she whispered. 'Hello, my little Adolf . . .'

'Ssshh!' said the innkeeper's wife. 'Listen! I think your husband is coming.'

The doctor walked over to the door and opened it and looked out into the corridor.

'Herr Hitler?'

'Yes.'

'Come in, please.'

A small man in a dark-green uniform stepped softly into the room and looked around him.

'Congratulations,' the doctor said. 'You have a son.'

The man had a pair of enormous whiskers meticulously groomed after the manner of the Emperor Franz Josef, and he smelled strongly of beer. 'A son?'

'Yes.'

'How is he?'

'He is fine. So is your wife.'

'Good.' The father turned and walked with a curious little prancing stride over to the bed where his wife was lying. 'Well, Klara,' he said, smiling through his whiskers. 'How did it go?' He bent down to take a look at the baby. Then he bent lower. In a series of quick jerky movements, he bent lower and lower until his face was only about twelve inches from the baby's head. The wife lay sideways on the pillow, staring up at him with a kind of supplicating look.

'He has the most marvellous pair of lungs,' the innkeeper's wife announced. 'You should have heard him screaming just after he came into this world.'

'But my God, Klara . . .'

'What is it, dear?'

'This one is even smaller than Otto was!'

The doctor took a couple of quick paces forward. 'There is nothing wrong with that child,' he said.

Slowly, the husband straightened up and turned away from the bed and looked at the doctor. He seemed bewildered and stricken. 'It's no good lying, Doctor,' he said. 'I know what it means. It's going to be the same all over again.'

'Now you listen to me,' the doctor said.

'But do you *know* what happened to the others, Doctor?'

'You must forget about the others, Herr Hitler. Give this one a chance.'

'But so small and weak!'

'My dear sir, he has only just been born.'

'Even so . . .'

'What are you trying to do?' cried the innkeeper's wife. 'Talk him into his grave?'

'That's enough!' the doctor said sharply.

The mother was weeping now. Great sobs were shaking her body.

The doctor walked over to the husband and put a hand on his shoulder. 'Be good to her,' he whispered. 'Please. It is very important.' Then he squeezed the husband's shoulder hard and began pushing him forward surreptitiously to the edge of the bed. The husband hesitated. The doctor squeezed harder, signalling to him urgently through fingers and thumb. At last, reluctantly, the husband bent down and kissed his wife lightly on the cheek.

'All right, Klara,' he said. 'Now stop crying.'

'I have prayed so hard that he will live, Alois.'

'Yes.'

'Every day for months I have gone to the church and begged on my knees that this one will be allowed to live.'

'Yes, Klara, I know.'

'Three dead children is all that I can stand, don't you realize that?'

'Of course.'

'He *must* live, Alois. He *must*, he *must* . . . Oh God, be merciful unto him now . . .'

# Claud's Dog

First published in *Someone Like You* (1953)

## *Mr Feasey*

We were both up early when the big day came.

I wandered into the kitchen for a shave, but Claud got dressed right away and went outside to arrange about the straw. The kitchen was a front room and through the window I could see the sun just coming up behind the line of trees on top of the ridge the other side of the valley.

Each time Claud came past the window with an armload of straw I noticed over the rim of the mirror the intent, breathless expression on his face, the great round bullet-head thrusting forward and the forehead wrinkled into deep corrugations right up to the hairline. I'd only seen this look on him once before and that was the evening he'd asked Clarice to marry him. Today he was so excited he even walked funny, treading softly as though the concrete around the filling-station were a shade too hot for the soles of his feet; and he kept packing more and more straw into the back of the van to make it comfortable for Jackie.

Then he came into the kitchen to get breakfast, and I watched him put the pot of soup on the stove and begin stirring it. He had a long metal spoon and he kept on stirring and stirring all the time it was coming to the boil, and about every half-minute he leaned forward and stuck his nose into that sickly-sweet steam of cooking horseflesh. Then he started putting extras into it – three peeled onions, a few young carrots, a cupful of stinging-nettle tops, a teaspoon of Valentine's Meat Juice, twelve drops of cod-liver oil – and everything he touched was handled very gently with the ends of his big fat fingers as though it might have been a little fragment of Venetian glass. He took some minced horsemeat from the icebox, measured one handful into Jackie's bowl, three into the other, and when the soup was ready he shared it out between the two, pouring it over the meat.

It was the same ceremony I'd seen performed each morning for the past five months, but never with such intense and breathless concentration as this. There was no talk, not even a glance my way, and when he turned and went out again to fetch the dogs, even the back of his neck and the shoulders seemed to be whispering. 'Oh Jesus, don't let anything go wrong, and especially don't let me *do* anything wrong today.'

I heard him talking softly to the dogs in the pen as he put the leashes on them, and when he brought them around into the kitchen, they came in prancing and pulling to get at the breakfast, treading up and down with their front feet and waving their enormous tails from side to side, like whips.

'All right,' Claud said, speaking at last. 'Which is it?'

Most mornings he'd offer to bet me a pack of cigarettes, but there were bigger things at stake today and I knew all he wanted for the moment was a little extra reassurance.

He watched me as I walked once around the two beauti-ful, identical, tall, velvety-black dogs, and he moved aside, holding the leashes at arm's length to give me a better view.

'Jackie!' I said, trying the old trick that never worked. 'Hey, Jackie!' Two identical heads with identical expressions flicked around to look at me, four bright, identical, deep-yellow eyes stared into mine. There'd been a time when I fancied the eyes of one were slightly darker yellow than those of the other. There'd also been a time when I thought I could recognize Jackie because of a deeper brisket and a shade more muscle on the hindquarters. But it wasn't so.

'Come on,' Claud said. He was hoping that today of all days I would make a bad guess.

'This one,' I said. 'This is Jackie.'

'Which?'

'This one on the left.'

'There!' he cried, his whole face suddenly beaming. 'You're wrong again!'

'I don't think I'm wrong.'

'You're about as wrong as you could possibly be. And now listen, Gordon, and I'll tell you something. All these last weeks, every morning while you've been trying to pick him out – you know what?'

'What?'

'I've been keeping count. And the result is you haven't been right even *one half* the time! You'd have done better tossing a coin!'

What he meant was that if I (who saw them every day and side by side) couldn't do it, why the hell should we be frightened of Mr Feasey? Claud knew Mr Feasey was famous for spotting ringers, but he knew also that it could be very difficult to tell the difference between two dogs when there wasn't any.

He put the bowls of food on the floor, giving Jackie the one with the least meat because he was running today. When he stood back to watch them eat, the shadow of deep concern was back again on his face and the large pale eyes were staring at Jackie with the same rapt and melting look of love that up till recently had been reserved only for Clarice.

'You see, Gordon,' he said. 'It's just what I've always told you. For the last hundred years there's been all manner of ringers, some good and some bad, but in the whole history of dog-racing there's never been a ringer like this.'

'I hope you're right,' I said, and my mind began travelling back to that freezing afternoon just before Christmas, four months ago, when Claud had asked to borrow the van and had driven away in the direction of Aylesbury without saying where he was going. I had assumed he was off to see Clarice, but late in the afternoon he had returned, bringing with him this dog he said he'd bought off a man for thirty-five shillings.

'Is he fast?' I had said. We were standing out by the pumps and Claud was holding the dog on a leash and looking at him, and a few snowflakes were falling and settling on the dog's back. The motor of the van was still running.

'Fast!' Claud had said. 'He's just about the slowest dog you ever saw in your whole life!'

'Then what you buy him for?'

'Well,' he had said, the big bovine face secret and

cunning, 'it occurred to me that maybe he might possibly look a little bit like Jackie. What d'you think?'

'I suppose he does a bit, now you come to mention it.'

He had handed me the leash and I had taken the new dog inside to dry him off while Claud had gone round to the pen to fetch his beloved. And when he returned and we put the two of them together for the first time, I can remember him stepping back and saying, 'Oh Jesus!' and standing dead still in front of them like he was seeing a phantom. Then he became very quick and quiet. He got down on his knees and began comparing them carefully point by point, and it was almost like the room was getting warmer and warmer the way I could feel his excitement growing every second through this long silent examination in which even the toenails and the dewclaws, eighteen on each dog, were matched alongside one another for colour.

'Look,' he said at last, standing up. 'Walk them up and down the room a few times, will you?' And then he had stayed there for quite five or six minutes leaning against the stove with his eyes half closed and his head on one side, watching them and frowning and chewing his lips. After that, as though he didn't believe what he had seen the first time, he had gone down again on his knees to recheck everything once more; but suddenly, in the middle of it, he had jumped up and looked at me, his face fixed and tense, with a curious whiteness around the nostrils and the eyes. 'All right,' he had said, a little tremor in his voice. 'You know what? We're home. We're rich.'

And then the secret conferences between us in the kitchen, the detailed planning, the selection of the most suitable track, and finally every other Saturday, eight times in all, locking up my filling-station (losing a whole afternoon's custom) and driving the ringer all the way up to Oxford to a scruffy little track out in the fields near Headington where the big money was played but which was actually nothing except a line of old posts and cord to mark the course, an upturned bicycle for pulling the dummy hare, and at the far end, in the distance, six traps and the starter. We had driven this ringer up there eight times over a period of sixteen weeks and entered him with Mr Feasey and stood around on the edge of the crowd in freezing raining cold, waiting for his name to go up on the blackboard in chalk. The Black Panther we called him. And when his time came, Claud would always lead him down to the traps and I would stand at the finish to catch him and keep him clear of the fighters, the gipsy dogs that the gipsies so often slipped in specially to tear another one to pieces at the end of a race.

But you know, there was something rather sad about taking this dog all the way up there so many times and letting him run and watching him and hoping and praying that whatever happened he would always come last. Of course the praying wasn't necessary and we never really had a moment's worry because the old fellow simply couldn't gallop and that's all there was to it. He ran exactly like a crab. The only time he didn't come last was when a big fawn dog by the name of Amber Flash put his foot in a hole and broke a hock and finished on three legs. But even then ours only just beat him. So this way we got him right down to bottom grade with the scrubbers, and the last time we were there all the bookies were laying him twenty or thirty to one and calling his name and begging people to back him.

Now at last, on this sunny April day, it was Jackie's turn to go instead. Claud said we mustn't run the ringer any more or Mr Feasey might begin to get tired of him and throw him out altogether, he was so slow. Claud said this was the exact psychological time to have it off, and that Jackie would win it anything between thirty and fifty lengths.

He had raised Jackie from a pup and the dog was only fifteen months now, but he was a good fast runner. He'd never raced yet, but we knew he was fast from clocking him round the little private schooling track at Uxbridge where Claud had taken him every Sunday since he was seven months old – except once when he was having some inoculations, Claud said he probably wasn't fast enough to win top grade at Mr Feasey's, but where we'd got him now, in bottom grade with the scrubbers, he could fall over and get up again and still win it twenty – well, anyway, ten or fifteen lengths, Claud said.

So all I had to do this morning was go to the bank in the village and draw out fifty pounds for myself and fifty for Claud which I would lend him as an advance against wages, and then at twelve o'clock lock up the filling-station and hang the notice on one of the pumps saying GONE FOR THE DAY. Claud would shut the ringer in the pen at the back and put Jackie in the van and off we'd go. I won't say I was as excited as Claud, but there again, I didn't have all sorts of important things depending on it either, like buying a house and being able to get married. Nor was I almost *born* in a kennel with greyhounds like he was, walking about thinking of absolutely nothing else all day – except perhaps Clarice in the evenings. Personally, I had my own career as a filling-station owner to keep me busy, not to mention second-hand cars, but if Claud wanted to fool around with dogs that was all right with me, especially a thing like today – if it came off. As a matter of fact, I don't mind admitting that every time I thought about the money we were putting on and the money we might win, my stomach gave a little lurch.

The dogs had finished their breakfast now and Claud took them out for a short walk across the field opposite while I got dressed and fried the eggs. Afterwards, I went to the bank and drew out the money (all in ones), and the rest of the morning seemed to go very quickly serving customers.

At twelve sharp I locked up and hung the notice on the pump. Claud came around from the back leading Jackie and carrying a large suitcase made of reddish-brown cardboard.

'Suitcase?'

'For the money,' Claud answered. 'You said yourself no man can carry two thousand pounds in his pockets.'

It was a lovely yellow spring day with the buds bursting all along the hedges and the sun shining through the new pale-green leaves on the big beech tree across the road. Jackie looked wonderful, with two big hard muscles the size of melons bulging on his hindquarters, his coat glistening like black velvet. While Claud was putting the suitcase in the van, the dog did a little prancing jig on his toes to show how fit he was, then he looked up at me and grinned, just like he knew he was off to the races to win two thousand pounds and a heap of glory. This Jackie had the widest most human-smiling grin I ever saw. Not only did he lift his upper lip, but he actually stretched the corners of his mouth so you could see every tooth in his head except perhaps one or two of the molars right at the back; and every time I saw him do it I found myself waiting to hear him start laughing out loud as well.

We got in the van and off we went. I was doing the driving. Claud was beside me and Jackie was standing up on the straw in the rear looking over our shoulders through the windshield. Claud kept turning round and trying to make him lie down so he wouldn't get thrown whenever we went round the sharp corners, but the dog was too excited to do anything except grin back at him and wave his enormous tail.

'You got the money, Gordon?' Claud was chain-smoking cigarettes and quite unable to sit still.

'Yes.'

'Mine as well?'

'I got a hundred and five altogether. Five for the winder like you said, so he won't stop the hare and make it a no-race.'

'Good,' Claud said, rubbing his hands together hard as though he were freezing cold. 'Good, good, good.'

We drove through the little narrow High Street of Great Missenden and caught a glimpse of old Rummins going into the Nag's Head for his morning pint, then outside the village we turned left and climbed over the ridge of the

Chilterns towards Princes Risborough, and from there it would only be twenty-odd miles to Oxford.

And now a silence and a kind of tension began to come over us both. We sat very quiet, not speaking at all, each nursing his own fears and excitements, containing his anxiety. And Claud kept smoking his cigarettes and throwing them half finished out the window. Usually, on these trips, he talked his head off all the way there and back, all the things he'd done with dogs in his life, the jobs he'd pulled, the places he'd been, the money he'd won; and all the things other people had done with dogs, the thievery, the cruelty, the unbelievable trickery and cunning of owners at the flapping tracks. But today I don't think he was trusting himself to speak very much. At this point, for that matter, nor was I. I was sitting there watching the road and trying to keep my mind off the immediate future by thinking back on all that stuff Claud had told me about this curious greyhound-racing racket.

I swear there wasn't a man alive who knew more about it than Claud did, and ever since we'd got the ringer and decided to pull this job, he'd taken it upon himself to give me an education in the business. By now, in theory at any rate, I suppose I knew nearly as much as him.

It had started during the very first strategy conference we'd had in the kitchen. I can remember it was the day after the ringer arrived and we were sitting there watching for customers through the window, and Claud was explaining to me all about what we'd have to do, and I was trying to follow him as best I could until finally there came one question I had to ask.

'What I don't see,' I had said, 'is why you use the ringer

at all. Wouldn't it be safer if we use Jackie all the time and simply stop him the first half-dozen races so he comes last? Then when we're good and ready, we can let him go. Same result in the end, wouldn't it be, if we do it right? And no danger of being caught.'

Well, as I say, that did it. Claud looked up at me quickly and he said, 'Hey! None of that! I'd just like you to know "stopping's" something I never do. What's come over you, Gordon?' He seemed genuinely pained and shocked by what I had said.

'I don't see anything wrong with it.'

'Now, listen to me, Gordon. Stopping a good dog breaks his heart. A good dog knows he's fast, and seeing all the others out there in front and not being able to catch them – it breaks his heart, I tell you. And what's more, you wouldn't be making suggestions like that if you knew some of the tricks them fellers do to stop their dogs at the flapping tracks.'

'Such as what, for example?' I had asked.

'Such as anything in the world almost, so long as it makes the dog go slower. And it takes a lot of stopping, a good greyhound does. Full of guts and so mad keen you can't even let them watch a race they'll tear the leash right out of your hand raring to go. Many's the time I've seen one with a broken leg insisting on finishing the race.'

He had paused then, looking at me thoughtfully with those large pale eyes, serious as hell and obviously thinking deep. 'Maybe,' he had said, 'if we're going to do this job properly I'd better tell you a thing or two so's you'll know what we're up against.'

'Go ahead and tell me,' I had said. 'I'd like to know.'

For a moment he stared in silence out the window. 'The main thing you got to remember,' he had said darkly, 'is that all these fellers going to the flapping tracks with dogs – they're artful. They're more artful than you could possibly imagine.' Again he paused, marshalling his thoughts.

'Now take for example the different ways of stopping a dog. The first, the commonest, is strapping.'

'Strapping?'

'Yes. Strapping 'em up. That's commonest. Pulling the muzzle-strap tight around their necks so they can't hardly breathe, see. A clever man knows just which hole on the strap to use and just how many lengths it'll take off his dog in a race. Usually a couple of notches is good for five or six lengths. Do it up real tight and he'll come last. I've known plenty of dogs collapse and die from being strapped up tight on a hot day. Strangulated, absolutely strangulated, and a very nasty thing it was too. Then again, some of 'em just tie two of the toes together with black cotton. Dog never runs well like that. Unbalances him.'

'That doesn't sound too bad.'

'Then there's others that put a piece of fresh-chewed gum up under their tails, right up close where the tail joins the body. And there's nothing funny about that,' he had said, indignant. 'The tail of a running dog goes up and down ever so slightly and the gum on the tail keeps sticking to the hairs on the backside, just where it's tenderest. No dog likes that, you know. Then there's sleeping pills. That's used a lot nowadays. They do it by weight, exactly like a doctor, and they measure the powder according to whether they want to slow him up five or ten or fifteen lengths. Those are just a few of the ordinary ways,' he had said. 'Actually they're nothing. Absolutely nothing, compared with some of the other things that's done to hold a dog back in a race, especially by the gipsies. There's things the gipsies do that are almost too disgusting to mention, such as when they're just putting the dog in the trap, things you wouldn't hardly do to your worst enemies.'

And when he had told me about those – which were, indeed, terrible things because they had to do with physical injury, quickly, painfully inflicted – then he had gone on to tell me what they did when they wanted the dog to win.

'There's just as terrible things done to make 'em go fast as to make 'em go slow,' he had said softly, his face veiled and secret. 'And perhaps the commonest of all is wintergreen. Whenever you see a dog going around with no hair on his back or little bald patches all over him – that's wintergreen. Just before the race they rub it hard into the skin. Sometimes it's Sloan's Liniment, but mostly it's wintergreen. Stings terrible. Stings so bad that all the old dog wants to do is run, run, run as fast as he possibly can to get away from the pain.

'Then there's special drugs they give with the needle. Mind you, that's the modern method and most of the spivs at the track are too ignorant to use it. It's the fellers coming down from London in the big cars with stadium dogs they've borrowed for the day by bribing the trainer – they're the ones who use the needle.'

I could remember him sitting there at the kitchen table

with a cigarette dangling from his mouth and dropping his eyelids to keep out the smoke and looking at me through his wrinkled, nearly closed eyes, and saying, 'What you've got to remember, Gordon, is this. There's nothing they won't do to make a dog win if they want him to. On the other hand, no dog can run faster than he's built, no matter what they do to him. So if we can get Jackie down into bottom grade, then we're home. No dog in bottom grade can get near him, not even with wintergreen and needles. Not even with ginger.'

'Ginger?'

'Certainly. That's a common one, ginger is. What they do, they take a piece of raw ginger about the size of a walnut, and about five minutes before the off they slip it into the dog.'

'You mean in his mouth? He eats it?'

'No,' he had said. 'Not in his mouth.'

And so it had gone on. During each of the eight long trips we had subsequently made to the track with the ringer I had heard more and more about this charming sport – more, especially, about the methods of stopping them and making them go (even the names of the drugs and the quantities to use). I heard about 'The rat treatment' (for non-chasers, to make them chase the dummy hare), where a rat is placed in a can which is then tied around the dog's neck. There's a small hole in the lid of the can just large enough for the rat to poke its head out and nip the dog. But the dog can't get at the rat, and so naturally he goes half crazy running around and being bitten in the neck, and the more he shakes the can the more the rat bites him.

Finally, someone releases the rat, and the dog, who up to then was a nice docile tail-wagging animal who wouldn't hurt a mouse, pounces on it in a rage and tears it to pieces. Do this a few times, Claud had said – 'Mind you, I don't hold with it myself' – and the dog becomes a real killer who will chase anything, even the dummy hare.

We were over the Chilterns now and running down out of the beechwoods into the flat elm- and oak-tree country south of Oxford. Claud sat quietly beside me, nursing his nervousness and smoking cigarettes, and every two or three minutes he would turn round to see if Jackie was all right. The dog was at last lying down, and each time Claud turned round, he whispered something to him softly, and the dog acknowledged his words with a faint movement of the tail that made the straw rustle.

Soon we would be coming into Thame, the broad High Street where they penned the pigs and cows and sheep on market day, and where the fair came once a year with the swings and roundabouts and bumping cars and gipsy caravans right there in the street in the middle of the town. Claud was born in Thame, and we'd never driven through it yet without him mentioning the fact.

'Well,' he said as the first houses came into sight, 'here's Thame. I was born and bred in Thame, you know, Gordon.'

'You told me.'

'Lots of funny things we used to do around here when we was nippers,' he said, slightly nostalgic.

'I'm sure.'

He paused, and I think more to relieve the tension

building up inside him than anything else, he began talking about the years of his youth.

'There was a boy next door,' he said. 'Gilbert Gomm his name was. Little sharp ferrety face and one leg a bit shorter'n the other. Shocking things him and me used to do together. You know one thing we done, Gordon?'

'What?'

'We'd go into the kitchen Saturday nights when Mum and Dad were at the pub, and we'd disconnect the pipe from the gas-ring and bubble the gas into a milk bottle full of water. Then we'd sit down and drink it out of teacups.'

'Was that so good?'

'Good! It was absolutely disgusting! But we'd put lashings of sugar in and then it didn't taste so bad.'

'Why did you drink it?'

Claud turned and looked at me, incredulous. 'You mean you never drunk "Snakes Water"!'

'Can't say I have.'

'I thought everyone done that when they was kids! It intoxicates you, just like wine only worse, depending on how long you let the gas bubble through. We used to get reeling drunk together there in the kitchen Saturday nights and it was marvellous. Until one night Dad comes home early and catches us. I'll never forget that night as long as I live. There was me holding the milk bottle, and the gas bubbling through it lovely, and Gilbert kneeling on the floor ready to turn off the tap the moment I give the word, and in walks Dad.'

'What did he say?'

'Oh Christ, Gordon, that was terrible. He didn't say

one word, but he stands there by the door and he starts feeling for his belt, undoing the buckle very slow and pulling the belt slow out of his trousers, looking at me all the time. Great big feller he was, with great big hands like coal hammers and a black moustache and them little purple veins running all over his cheeks. Then he comes over quick and grabs me by the coat and lets me have it, hard as he can, using the end with the buckle on it and, honest to God, Gordon, I thought he was going to kill me. But in the end he stops and then he puts on the belt again, slow and careful, buckling it up and tucking in the flap and belching with the beer he'd drunk. And then he walks out again back to the pub, still without saying a word. Worst hiding I ever had in my life.'

'How old were you then?'

'Round about eight, I should think,' Claud said.

As we drew closer to Oxford, he became silent again. He kept twisting his neck to see if Jackie was all right, to touch him, to stroke his head, and once he turned around and knelt on the seat to gather more straw around the dog, murmuring something about a draught. We drove around the fringe of Oxford and into a network of narrow open country roads, and after a while we turned into a small bumpy lane and along this we began to overtake a thin stream of men and women all walking and cycling in the same direction. Some of the men were leading greyhounds. There was a large saloon car in front of us and through the rear window we could see a dog sitting on the back seat between two men.

'They come from all over,' Claud said darkly. 'That one

there's probably come up special from London. Probably slipped him out from one of the big stadium kennels just for the afternoon. That could be a Derby dog probably, for all we know.'

'Hope he's not running against Jackie.'

'Don't worry,' Claud said. 'All new dogs automatically go in top grade. That's one rule Mr Feasey's very particular about.'

There was an open gate leading into a field, and Mr Feasey's wife came forward to take our admission money before we drove in.

'He'd have her winding the bloody pedals too if she had the strength,' Claud said. 'Old Feasey don't employ more people than he has to.'

I drove across the field and parked at the end of a line of cars along the top hedge. We both got out and Claud went quickly round the back to fetch Jackie. I stood beside the car, waiting. It was a very large field with a steepish slope on it and we were at the top of the slope, looking down. In the distance I could see the six starting-traps and the wooden posts marking the track which ran along the bottom of the field and turned sharp at right angles and came on up the hill towards the crowd, to the finish. Thirty yards beyond the finishing line stood the upturned bicycle for driving the hare. Because it is portable, this is the standard machine for hare-driving used at all flapping tracks. It comprises a flimsy wooden platform about eight feet high, supported on four poles knocked into the ground. On top of the platform there is fixed, upside down with wheels in the air, an ordinary old bicycle. The rear wheel is to the front, facing down the track, and from it the tyre has been removed, leaving a concave metal rim. One end of the cord that pulls the hare is attached to this rim, and the winder (or hare-driver), by straddling the bicycle at the back and turning the pedals with his hands, revolves the wheel and winds in the cord around the rim. This pulls the dummy hare towards him at any speed he likes up to forty miles an hour. After each race someone takes the dummy hare (with cord attached) all the way down to the starting traps again, thus unwinding the cord on the wheel, ready for a fresh start. From his high platform, the winder can watch the race and regulate the speed of the hare to keep it just ahead of the leading dog. He can also stop the hare any time he wants and make it a 'no-race' (if the wrong dog looks like winning) by suddenly turning the pedals backwards and getting the cord tangled up in the hub of the wheel. The other way of doing it is to slow down the hare suddenly, for perhaps one second, and that makes the lead dog automatically check a little so that the others catch up with him. He is an important man, the winder.

I could see Mr Feasey's winder already standing atop his platform, a powerful-looking man in a blue sweater, leaning on the bicycle and looking down at the crowd through the smoke of his cigarette.

There is a curious law in England which permits race meetings of this kind to be held only seven times a year over one piece of ground. That is why all Mr Feasey's equipment was movable, and after the seventh meeting he would simply transfer to the next field. The law didn't bother him at all.

There was already a good crowd and the bookmakers

were erecting their stands in a line over to the right. Claud had Jackie out of the van now and was leading him over to a group of people clustered around a small stocky man dressed in riding-breeches – Mr Feasey himself. Each person in the group had a dog on a leash and Mr Feasey kept writing names in a notebook that he held folded in his left hand. I sauntered over to watch.

'Which you got there?' Mr Feasey said, pencil poised above the notebook.

'Midnight,' a man said who was holding a black dog.

Mr Feasey stepped back a pace and looked most carefully at the dog.

'Midnight. Right. I got him down.'

'Jane,' the next man said.

'Let me look. Jane . . . Jane . . . yes, all right.'

'Soldier.' This dog was led by a tall man with long teeth who wore a dark-blue, double-breasted lounge suit, shiny with wear, and when he said 'Soldier' he began slowly to scratch the seat of his trousers with the hand that wasn't holding the leash.

Mr Feasey bent down to examine the dog. The other man looked up at the sky.

'Take him away,' Mr Feasey said.

The man looked down quick and stopped scratching.

'Go on, take him away.'

'Listen, Mr Feasey,' the man said, lisping slightly through his long teeth. 'Now don't talk so bloody silly, *please*.'

'Go on and beat it, Larry, and stop wasting my time. You know as well as I do the Soldier's got two white toes on his off fore.'

'Now look, Mr Feasey,' the man said. 'You ain't even seen Soldier for six months at least.'

'Come on now, Larry, and beat it. I haven't got time arguing with you.' Mr Feasey didn't appear the least angry. 'Next,' he said.

I saw Claud step forward leading Jackie. The large bovine face was fixed and wooden, the eyes staring at something about a yard above Mr Feasey's head, and he was holding the leash so tight his knuckles were like a row of little white onions. I knew just how he was feeling. I felt the same way myself at that moment, and it was even worse when Mr Feasey suddenly started laughing.

'Hey!' he cried. 'Here's the Black Panther. Here's the champion.'

'That's right, Mr Feasey,' Claud said.

'Well, I'll tell you,' Mr Feasey said, still grinning. 'You can take him right back home where he come from. I don't want him.'

'But look here, Mr Feasey . . .'

'Six or eight times at least I've run him for you now and that's enough. Look – why don't you shoot him and have done with it?'

'Now, listen, Mr Feasey, *please*. Just once more and I'll never ask you again.'

'Not even once! I got more dogs than I can handle here today. There's no room for crabs like that.'

I thought Claud was going to cry.

'Now honest, Mr Feasey,' he said. 'I been up at six every morning this past two weeks giving him roadwork and massage and buying him beefsteaks, and believe me he's a different dog absolutely than what he was last time he run.'

The words 'different dog' caused Mr Feasey to jump like he'd been pricked with a hatpin. 'What's that!' he cried. 'Different dog!'

I'll say this for Claud, he kept his head. 'See here, Mr Feasey,' he said. 'I'll thank you not to go implying things to me. You know very well I didn't mean that.'

'All right, all right. But just the same, you can take him away. There's no sense running dogs as slow as him. Take him home now, will you please, and don't hold up the whole meeting.'

I was watching Claud. Claud was watching Mr Feasey. Mr Feasey was looking round for the next dog to enter up. Under his brown tweedy jacket he wore a yellow pullover, and this streak of yellow on his breast and his thin gaitered legs and the way he jerked his head from side to side made him seem like some sort of a little perky bird – a goldfinch, perhaps.

Claud took a step forward. His face was beginning to purple slightly with the outrage of it all and I could see his Adam's apple moving up and down as he swallowed.

'I'll tell you what I'll do, Mr Feasey. I'm so absolutely sure this dog's improved I'll bet you a quid he don't finish last. There you are.'

Mr Feasey turned slowly around and looked at Claud. 'You crackers?' he asked.

'I'll bet you a quid, there you are, just to prove what I'm saying.'

It was a dangerous move, certain to cause suspicion,

but Claud knew it was the only thing left to do. There was silence while Mr Feasey bent down and examined the dog. I could see the way his eyes were moving slowly over the animal's whole body, part by part. There was something to admire in the man's thoroughness, and in his memory; something to fear also in this self-confident little rogue who held in his head the shape and colour and markings of perhaps several hundred different but very similar dogs. He never needed more than one little clue – a small scar, a splay toe, a trifle in at the hocks, a less pronounced wheelback, a slightly darker brindle – Mr Feasey always remembered.

So I watched him now as he bent down over Jackie. His face was pink and fleshy, the mouth small and tight as though it couldn't stretch enough to make a smile, and the eyes were like two little cameras focused sharply on the dog.

'Well,' he said, straightening up. 'It's the same dog, anyway.'

'I should hope so too!' Claud cried. 'Just what sort of a fellow you think I am, Mr Feasey?'

'I think you're crackers, that's what I think. But it's a nice easy way to make a quid. I suppose you forgot how Amber Flash nearly beat him on three legs last meeting?'

'This one wasn't fit then,' Claud said. 'He hadn't had beefsteak and massage and roadwork like I've been giving him lately. But look, Mr Feasey, you're not to go sticking him in top grade just to win the bet. This is a bottom-grade dog, Mr Feasey. You know that.'

Mr Feasey laughed. The small button mouth opened

into a tiny circle and he laughed and looked at the crowd, who laughed with him. 'Listen,' he said, laying a hairy hand on Claud's shoulder. 'I know my dogs. I don't have to do any fiddling around to win *this* quid. He goes in bottom.'

'Right,' Claud said. 'That's a bet.' He walked away with Jackie and I joined him.

'Jesus, Gordon, that was a near one!'

'Shook me.'

'But we're in now,' Claud said. He had that breathless look on his face again and he was walking about quick and funny, like the ground was burning his feet.

People were still coming through the gate into the field and there were easily three hundred of them now. Not a very nice crowd. Sharp-nosed men and women with dirty faces and bad teeth and quick shifty eyes. The dregs of the big town. Oozing out like sewage from a cracked pipe and trickling along the road through the gate and making a smelly little pond of sewage at the top end of the field. They were all there, all the spivs, and the gipsies and the touts and the dregs and the sewage and the scraping and the scum from the cracked drainpipes of the big town. Some with dogs, some without. Dogs led about on pieces of string, miserable dogs with hanging heads, thin mangy dogs with sores on their quarters (from sleeping on board), sad old dogs with grey muzzles, doped dogs, dogs stuffed with porridge to stop them winning, dogs walking stiff-legged – one especially, a white one. 'Claud, why is that white one walking so stiff-legged?'

'Which one?'

'That one over there.'

'Ah. Yes, I see. Very probably because he's been hung.'

'Hung?'

'Yes, hung. Suspended in a harness for twenty-four hours with his legs dangling.'

'Good God, but why?'

'To make him run slow, of course. Some people don't hold with dope or stuffing or strapping up. So they hang 'em.'

'I see.'

'Either that,' Claud said, 'or they sandpaper them. Rub their pads with rough sandpaper and take the skin off so it hurts when they run.'

'Yes, I see.'

And then the fitter, brighter-looking dogs, the better-fed ones who get horsemeat every day, not pig-swill or rusk and cabbage water, their coats shinier, their tails moving, pulling at their leads, undoped, unstuffed, awaiting perhaps a more unpleasant fate, the muzzle-strap to be tightened an extra four notches. *But make sure he can breathe now, Jock. Don't choke him completely. Don't let's have him collapse in the middle of the race. Just so he wheezes a bit, see. Go on tightening it up an extra notch at a time until you can hear him wheezing. You'll see his mouth open and he'll start breathing heavy. Then it's just right, but not if his eyeballs is bulging. Watch out for that, will you? OK?*

*OK.*

'Let's get away from the crowd, Gordon. It don't do Jackie no good getting excited by all these other dogs.'

We walked up the slope to where the cars were parked,

then back and forth in front of the line of cars, keeping the dog on the move. Inside some of the cars I could see men sitting with their dogs, and the men scowled at us through the windows as we went by.

'Watch out now, Gordon. We don't want any trouble.'

'No, all right.'

These were the best dogs of all, the secret ones kept in the cars and taken out quick just to be entered up (under some invented name) and put back again quick and held there till the last minute, then straight down to the traps and back again into the cars after the race so no nosey bastard gets too close a look, The trainer at the big stadium said so. *All right, he said. You can have him, but for Christsake don't let anybody recognize him. There's thousands of people know this dog, so you've got to be careful, see. And it'll cost you fifty pound.*

Very fast dogs these, but it doesn't much matter how fast they are, they probably get the needle anyway, just to make sure. One and a half cc's of ether, subcutaneous, done in the car, injected very slow. That'll put ten lengths on any dog. Or sometimes it's caffeine in oil, or camphor. That makes them go too. The men in the big cars know all about that. And some of them know about whisky. But that's intravenous. Not so easy when it's intravenous. Might miss the vein. All you got to do is miss the vein and it don't work and where are you then? So it's ether, or it's caffeine, or it's camphor. *Don't give her too much of that stuff now, Jock. What does she weigh? Fifty-eight pounds. All right then, you know what the man told us. Wait a minute now. I got it written down on a piece of paper. Here it is. Point 1 of a cc per 10 pounds bodyweight equals 5 lengths over 300 yards. Wait a minute now while*

*I work it out. Oh Christ, you better guess it. Just guess it, Jock. It'll be all right you'll find. Shouldn't be any trouble anyway because I picked the others in the race myself. Cost me a tenner to old Feasey. A bloody tenner I gave him, and Dear Mr Feasey, I says, that's for your birthday and because I love you.*

*Thank you ever so much, Mr Feasey says. Thank you, my good and trusted friend.*

And for stopping them, for the men in the big cars, it's chlorbutol. That's a beauty, chlorbutol, because you can give it the night before, especially to someone else's dog. Or pethidine. Pethidine and hyoscine mixed, whatever that may be.

'Lot of fine old English sporting gentry here,' Claud said.

'Certainly are.'

'Watch your pockets, Gordon. You got that money hidden away?'

We walked around the back of the line of cars – between the cars and the hedge – and I saw Jackie stiffen and begin to pull forward on the leash, advancing with a stiff crouching tread. About thirty yards away there were two men. One was holding a large fawn greyhound, the dog stiff and tense like Jackie. The other was holding a sack in his hands.

'Watch,' Claud whispered, 'they're giving him a kill.'

Out of the sack on to the grass tumbled a small white rabbit, fluffy white, young, tame. It righted itself and sat still, crouching in the hunched-up way rabbits crouch, its nose close to the ground. A frightened rabbit. Out of the sack so suddenly on to the grass with such a bump. Into the bright light. The dog was going mad with excitement now, jumping up against the leash, pawing the ground, throwing himself forward, whining. The rabbit saw the dog. It drew in its head and stayed still, paralysed with fear. The man transferred his hold to the dog's collar, and the dog twisted and jumped and tried to get free. The other man pushed the rabbit with his foot but it was too terrified to move. He pushed it again, flicking it forward with his toe like a football, and the rabbit rolled over several times, righted itself and began to hop over the grass away from the dog. The other man released the dog, which pounced with one huge pounce upon the rabbit, and then came the squeals, not very loud but shrill and anguished and lasting rather a long time.

'There you are,' Claud said. 'That's a kill.'

'Not sure I liked it very much.'

'I told you before, Gordon. Most of 'em does it. Keens the dog up before a race.'

'I still don't like it.'

'Nor me. But they all do it. Even in the big stadiums the trainers do it. Proper barbary I call it.'

We strolled away and below us on the slope of the hill the crowd was thickening and the bookies' stands with the names written on them in red and gold and blue were all erected now in a long line back of the crowd, each bookie already stationed on an upturned box beside his stand, a pack of numbered cards in one hand, a piece of chalk in the other, his clerk behind him with book and pencil. Then we saw Mr Feasey walking over to a blackboard that was nailed to a post stuck in the ground.

'He's chalking up the first race,' Claud said. 'Come on, quick!'

We walked rapidly down the hill and joined the crowd. Mr Feasey was writing the runners on the blackboard, copying names from his soft-covered notebook, and a little hush of suspense fell upon the crowd as they watched.

1. Sally
2. Three Quid
3. Snailbox Lady
4. Black Panther
5. Whisky
6. Rockit

'He's in it!' Claud whispered. 'First race! Trap four! Now, listen, Gordon! Give me a fiver quick to show the winder.' Claud could hardly speak from excitement. That patch of whiteness had returned around his nose and eyes, and when I handed him a five-pound note, his whole arm was shaking as he took it. The man who was going to wind the bicycle pedals was still standing on top of the wooden platform in his blue jersey, smoking. Claud went over and stood below him, looking up.

'See this fiver,' he said, talking softly, holding it folded small in the palm of his hand.

The man glanced at it without moving his head.

'Just so long as you wind her true this race, see. No stopping and no slowing down and run her fast. Right?'

The man didn't move but there was a slight, almost imperceptible lifting of the eyebrows. Claud turned away.

'Now, look, Gordon. Get the money on gradual, all in

little bits like I told you. Just keep going down the line putting on little bits so you don't kill the price, see. And I'll be walking Jackie down very slow, as slow as I dare, to give you plenty of time. Right?'

'Right.'

'And don't forget to be standing ready to catch him at the end of the race. Get him clear away from all them others when they start fighting for the hare. Grab a hold of him tight and don't let go till I come running up with the collar and lead. That Whisky's a gipsy dog and he'll tear the leg off anything as gets in his way.'

'Right,' I said. 'Here we go.'

I saw Claud lead Jackie over to the finishing post and collect a yellow jacket with '4' written on it large. Also a muzzle. The other five runners were there too, the owners fussing around them, putting on their numbered jackets, adjusting their muzzles. Mr Feasey was officiating, hopping about in his tight riding-breeches like an anxious perky bird, and once I saw him say something to Claud and laugh. Claud ignored him. Soon they would all start to lead the dogs down the track, the long walk down the hill and across to the far corner of the field to the starting-traps. It would take them ten minutes to walk it. I've got at least ten minutes, I told myself, and then I began to push my way through the crowd standing six or seven deep in front of the line of bookies.

'Even money Whisky! Even money Whisky! Five to two Sally! Even money Whisky! Four to one Snailbox! Come on now! Hurry up, hurry up! Which is it?'

On every board all down the line the Black Panther was

chalked up at twenty-five to one. I edged forward to the nearest book.

'Three pounds Black Panther,' I said, holding out the money.

The man on the box had an inflamed magenta face and traces of some white substance around the corners of his mouth. He snatched the money and dropped it in his satchel. 'Seventy-five pounds to three Black Panther,' he said. 'Number forty-two.' He handed me a ticket and his clerk recorded the bet.

I stepped back and wrote rapidly on the back of the ticket '75 to 3', then slipped it into the inside pocket of my jacket with the money.

So long as I continued to spread the cash out thin like this, it ought to be all right. And anyway, on Claud's instructions, I'd made a point of betting a few pounds on the ringer every time he'd run so as not to arouse any suspicion when the real day arrived. Therefore, with some confidence, I went all the way down the line staking three pounds with each book. I didn't hurry, but I didn't waste any time either, and after each bet I wrote the amount on the back of the card before slipping it into my pocket. There were seventeen bookies. I had seventeen tickets and had laid out fifty-one pounds without disturbing the price one point. Forty-nine pounds left to get on. I glanced quickly down the hill. One owner and his dog had already reached the traps. The others were only twenty or thirty yards away. Except for Claud. Claud and Jackie were only halfway there. I could see Claud in his old khaki greatcoat sauntering slowly along with Jackie pulling ahead keenly

CLAUD'S DOG

on the leash, and once I saw him stop completely and bend down, pretending to pick something up. When he went on again he seemed to have developed a limp so as to go slower still. I hurried back to the other end of the line to start again.

'Three pounds Black Panther.'

The bookmaker, the one with the magenta face and the white substance around the mouth, glanced up sharply, remembering the last time, and in one swift almost graceful movement of the arm he licked his fingers and wiped the figure 25 neatly off the board. His wet fingers left a small dark patch opposite Black Panther's name.

'All right, you got one more seventy-five to three,' he said. 'But that's the lot.' Then he raised his voice and shouted, 'Fifteen to one Black Panther! Fifteens the Panther!'

All down the line the twenty-fives were wiped out and it was fifteen to one the Panther now. I took it quick, but by the time I was through the bookies had had enough and they weren't quoting him any more. They'd only taken six pounds each, but they stood to lose a hundred and fifty, and for them – small-time bookies at a little country flapping track – that was quite enough for one race, thank you very much. I felt pleased the way I'd managed it. Lots of tickets now. I took them out of my pockets and counted them and they were like a thin pack of cards in my hand. Thirty-three tickets in all. And what did we stand to win? Let me see . . . something over two thousand pounds. Claud had said he'd win it thirty lengths. Where was Claud now?

Far away down the hill I could see the khaki greatcoat standing by the traps and the big black dog alongside. All the other dogs were already in and the owners were beginning to walk away. Claud was bending down now, coaxing Jackie into number four, and then he was closing the door and turning away and beginning to run up the hill towards the crowd, the greatcoat flapping around him. He kept looking back over his shoulder as he ran.

Beside the traps the starter stood, and his hand was up waving a handkerchief. At the other end of the track, beyond the winning-post, quite close to where I stood, the man in the blue jersey was straddling the upturned bicycle on top of the wooden platform and he saw the signal and waved back and began to turn the pedals with his hands. Then a tiny white dot in the distance – the artificial hare that was in reality a football with a piece of white rabbit-skin tacked on to it – began to move away from the traps, accelerating fast. The traps went up and the dogs flew out. They flew out in a single dark lump, all together, as though it were one wide dog instead of six, and almost at once I saw Jackie drawing away from the field. I knew it was Jackie because of the colour. There weren't any other black dogs in the race. It was Jackie, all right. Don't move, I told myself. Don't move a muscle or an eyelid or a toe or a fingertip. Stand quite still and don't move. Watch him going. Come on, Jackson, boy! No, don't shout. It's unlucky to shout. And don't move. Be all over in twenty seconds. Round the sharp bend now and coming up the hill and he must be fifteen or twenty lengths clear. Easy twenty lengths. Don't count the lengths, it's unlucky. And don't move. Don't move your head. Watch him out of your eye-corners. Watch that Jackson go! He's really laying down to it now up that hill. He's won it now! He can't lose it now . . .

When I got over to him he was fighting the rabbit-skin and trying to pick it up in his mouth, but his muzzle wouldn't allow it, and the other dogs were pounding up behind him and suddenly they were all on top of him grabbing for the rabbit and I got hold of him round the neck and dragged him clear like Claud had said and knelt down on the grass and held him tight with both arms round his body. The other catchers were having a time all trying to grab their own dogs.

Then Claud was beside me, blowing heavily, unable to speak from blowing and excitement, removing Jackie's muzzle, putting on the collar and lead, and Mr Feasey was there too standing with hands on hips, the button mouth pursed up tight like a mushroom, the two little cameras staring at Jackie all over again.

'So that's the game, is it?' he said.

Claud was bending over the dog and acting like he hadn't heard.

'I don't want you here no more after this, you understand that?'

Claud went on fiddling with Jackie's collar.

I heard someone behind us saying, 'That flat-faced bastard swung it properly on old Feasey this time.' Someone else laughed. Mr Feasey walked away, Claud straightened up and went over with Jackie to the hare-driver in the blue jersey who had dismounted from his platform.

'Cigarette,' Claud said, offering the pack.

The man took one, also the five-pound note that was folded up small in Claud's fingers.

'Thanks,' Claud said. 'Thanks very much.'

'Don't mention,' the man said.

Then Claud turned to me. 'You get it all on, Gordon?' He was jumping up and down and rubbing his hands and patting Jackie, and his lips trembled as he spoke.

'Yes. Half at twenty-fives, half at fifteens.'

'Oh Christ, Gordon, that's marvellous. Wait here till I get the suitcase.'

'You take Jackie,' I said, 'and go and sit in the car. I'll see you later.'

There was nobody around the bookies now. I was the only one with anything to collect, and I walked slowly with a sort of dancing stride and a wonderful bursting feeling in my chest, towards the first one in the line, the man with the magenta face and the white substance on his mouth. I stood in front of him and I took all the time I wanted going through my pack of tickets to find the two that were his. The name was Syd Pratchett. It was written up large across his board in gold letters on a scarlet field – 'SYD PRATCHETT. THE BEST ODDS IN THE MIDLANDS. PROMPT SETTLEMENT.'

I handed him the first ticket and said, 'Seventy-eight pounds to come.' It sounded so good I said it again, making a delicious little song of it. 'Seventy-eight pounds to come on this one.' I didn't mean to gloat over Mr Pratchett. As a matter of fact. I was beginning to like him quite a lot. I even felt sorry for him having to fork out so much money. I hoped his wife and kids wouldn't suffer.

'Number forty-two,' Mr Pratchett said, turning to his clerk who held the big book. 'Forty-two wants seventy-eight pounds.'

There was a pause while the clerk ran his finger down the column of recorded bets. He did this twice, then he looked up at the boss and began to shake his head.

'No,' he said. 'Don't pay. That ticket backed Snailbox Lady.'

Mr Pratchett, standing on his box, leaned over and peered down at the book. He seemed to be disturbed by what the clerk had said, and there was a look of genuine concern on the huge magenta face.

The clerk is a fool, I thought, and any moment now Mr Pratchett's going to tell him so.

But when Mr Pratchett turned back to me, the eyes had become narrow and hostile. 'Now, look, Charley,' he said softly. 'Don't let's have any of that. You know very well you bet Snailbox. What's the idea?'

'I bet Black Panther,' I said. 'Two separate bets of three pounds each at twenty-five to one. Here's the second ticket.'

This time he didn't even bother to check it with the book. 'You bet Snailbox, Charley,' he said. 'I remember you coming round.' With that, he turned away from me and started wiping the names of the last race runners off his board with a wet rag. Behind him, the clerk had closed the book and was lighting himself a cigarette. I stood watching them, and I could feel the sweat beginning to break through the skin all over my body.

'Let me see the book.'

Mr Pratchett blew his nose in the wet rag and dropped it to the ground. 'Look,' he said, 'why don't you go away and stop annoying me?'

The point was this: a bookmaker's ticket, unlike a totalizator ticket, never has anything written on it regarding the nature of your bet. This is normal practice, the same at every racetrack in the country, whether it's the Silver Ring at Newmarket, the Royal Enclosure at Ascot, or a tiny country flapping track near Oxford. All you receive is a card bearing the bookie's name and a serial number. The wager is (or should be) recorded by the bookie's clerk in his book alongside the number of the ticket, but apart from that there is no evidence at all of how you betted.

'Go on,' Mr Pratchett was saying. 'Hop it.'

I stepped back a pace and glanced down the long line of bookmakers. None of them was looking my way. Each was standing motionless on his little wooden box beside his wooden placard, staring straight ahead into the crowd. I went up to the next one and presented a ticket.

'I had three pounds on Black Panther at twenty-five to one,' I said firmly. 'Seventy-eight pounds to come.'

This man, who had a soft inflamed face, went through exactly the same routine as Mr Pratchett, questioning his clerk, peering at the book, and giving me the same answers.

'Whatever's the matter with you?' he said quietly, speaking to me as though I were eight years old. 'Trying such a silly thing as that.'

This time I stepped well back. 'You dirty thieving bastards!' I cried. 'The whole lot of you!'

Automatically, as though they were puppets, all the

heads down the line flicked round and looked at me. The expressions didn't alter. It was just the heads that moved, all seventeen of them, and seventeen pairs of cold glassy eyes looked down at me. There was not the faintest flicker of interest in any of them.

'Somebody spoke,' they seemed to be saying. 'We didn't hear it. It's a nice day today.'

The crowd, sensing excitement, was beginning to move in around me. I ran back to Mr Pratchett, right up close to him, and poked him in the stomach with my finger. 'You're a thief! A lousy little thief!' I shouted.

The extraordinary thing was, Mr Pratchett didn't seem to resent this at all.

'Well, I never,' he said. '*Look* who's talking.'

Then suddenly the big face broke into a wide, frog-like grin, and he looked over at the crowd and shouted, '*Look* who's talking!'

All at once everybody started to laugh. Down the line the bookies were coming to life and turning to each other and laughing and pointing at me and shouting, '*Look* who's talking! *Look* who's talking!' The crowd began to take up the cry as well, and I stood there on the grass alongside Mr Pratchett with his wad of tickets as thick as a pack of cards in my hand, listening to them and feeling slightly hysterical. Over the heads of the people I could see Mr Feasey beside his blackboard, already chalking up the runners for the next race; and then beyond him, far away up the top of the field, I caught sight of Claud standing by the van, waiting for me with the suitcase in his hand.

It was time to go home.

# ROALD DAHL

Roald Dahl was a spy, ace fighter-pilot, chocolate historian and medical inventor. He was also the author of Charlie and the Chocolate Factory, Matilda, The BFG and many more brilliant stories. He remains the World's No.1 storyteller.

# CHARMING BAKER

Born in Hampshire 1964, Charming Baker spent much of his early life travelling around the world following his father, a commando in the British Army. At the age of twelve, he and his family finally settled in Ripon, North Yorkshire. Baker left school at sixteen and worked various manual jobs. In 1985, having gone back to college, he was accepted onto a course at the prestigious Central Saint Martin's, where he later returned as a lecturer. After graduating, Baker worked for many years as a commercial artist as well as developing his personal work.

Solo exhibitions include the Truman Brewery, London, 2007, Redchurch Street Gallery, London, 2009, New York Studio Gallery, NYC, 2010, Mercer Street, London, 2011 and Milk Studios, LA, 2013. Baker has also exhibited with the Fine Art Society, collaborated with Sir Paul Smith for a sculpture entitled 'Triumph in the Face of Absurdity', which was displayed at the Victoria and Albert Museum, and continues to be committed to creating work to raise money for many charities. He has recently been commissioned to be a presenter on *The Art Show*. His work is in many international collections.

Although Baker has produced sculptural pieces in a wide and varied choice of materials, as well as many large-scale and detailed drawings, he remains primarily a painter with an interest in narrative and an understanding of the tradition of painting. Known to purposefully damage his work by drilling, cutting and even shooting it, Baker intentionally puts in to question the preciousness of art and the definition of its beauty, adding to the emotive charge of the work he produces. Indeed Edward Lucie-Smith has described Baker's paintings as having, something more, a kind of romantic melancholy that is very British. And sometimes the melancholy turns out to have sharp claws. The pictures make you sit up and examine your conscience.

Charming Baker lives and works in London.

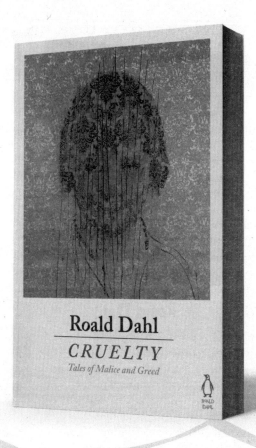

# CRUELTY
## *Tales of Malice and Greed*

---

Even when we mean to be kind we can sometimes be cruel. We each have a streak of nastiness inside us. In these ten tales of cruelty Roald Dahl explores how and why it is we make others suffer.

Among others, you'll read the story of two young bullies and the boy they torment, the adulterous wife who uncovers her husband's secret, the man with a painting tattooed on his back whose value he doesn't appreciate and the butler and chef who run rings around their obnoxious employer.

# DECEPTION
## *Tales of Intrigue and Lies*

Why do we lie? Why do we deceive those we love most? What do we fear revealing? In these ten tales of deception Roald Dahl explores our tireless efforts to hide the truth about ourselves.

Here, among many others tales you'll read about how to get away with the perfect murder, the old man whose wagers end in a most disturbing payment, how revenge is sweeter when it is carried out by someone else and the card sharp so good at cheating he does something surprising with his life.

Roald Dahl

*LUST*

*Tales of Craving and Desire*

# LUST
*Tales of Craving and Desire*

To what lengths would you go to achieve your heart's desire? In these ten tales of maddening lust Roald Dahl explores how our darkest impulses reveal who we really are.

Here you will read a story concerning wife swapping with a twist, hear of the aphrodisiac that drives men into a frenzy, discover the last act in a tale of jilted first love and discover the naked truth of art.

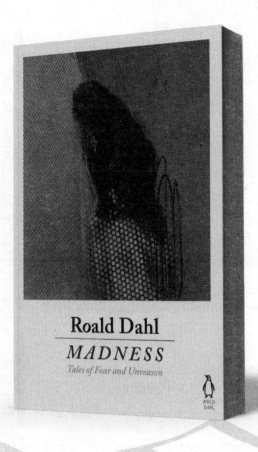

## MADNESS
*Tales of Fear and Unreason*

Our greatest fear is of losing control – above all, of losing control of ourselves. In these ten unsettling tales of unexpected madness Roald Dahl explores what happens when we let go of our sanity.

Among other stories, you'll meet the husband with a jealous fixation on the family cat, the landlady who wants her guests to stay forever, the man whose taste for pork leads him astray and the wife with a pathological fear of being late.

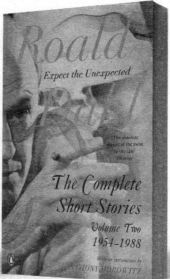

# THE COMPLETE ROALD DAHL
# SHORT STORIES VOL 1 & 2

*'They are brutal, these stories, and yet you finish reading each one with a smile, or maybe even a hollow laugh, certainly a shiver of gratification, because the conclusion always seems so right'*
**Charlie Higson**

In these two volumes chronologically collecting all Roald Dahl's 55 published adult short stories, written between 1944 and 1988, and introduced by Charlie Higson and Anthony Horowitz, we see Roald Dahl's powerful and dark imagination pen some of the most unsettling and disquieting tales ever written.

Whether you're young or old, once you've stepped into the brilliant, troubling world of Roald Dahl, you'll never be the same again.

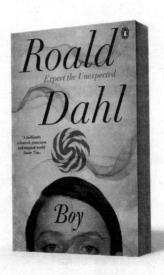

# BOY

---

*'An autobiography is a book a person writes about his own life and it is usually full of all sorts of boring details. This is not an autobiography. I would never write a history of myself. On the other hand, throughout my young days at school and just afterwards a number of things happened to me that I have never forgotten . . .'*

*Boy* is a funny, insightful and at times grotesque glimpse into the early life of Roald Dahl. We discover his experiences of the English public school system, the idyllic paradise of summer holidays in Norway, the pleasures (and pains) of the sweetshop, and how it is that he avoided being a Boazer.

This is the unadulterated childhood – sad and funny, macabre and delightful – which speaks of an age which vanished with the coming of the Second World War.

'A shimmering fabric of his yesterdays, the magic and the hurt' *Observer*

'As frightening and funny as his fiction' *The New York Times Book Review*

'Superbly written. A glimpse of a brilliant eccentric' *New Statesman*

# GOING SOLO

*'They did not think for one moment that they would find anything but a burnt-out fuselage and a charred skeleton, and they were astounded when they came upon my still-breathing body lying in the sand nearby.'*

In 1938 Roald Dahl was fresh out of school and bound for his first job in Africa, hoping to find adventure far from home. However, he got far more excitement than he bargained for when the outbreak of the Second World War led him to join the RAF. His account of his experiences in Africa, crashing a plane in the Western Desert, rescue and recovery from his horrific injuries in Alexandria, flying a Hurricane as Greece fell to the Germans, and many other daring deeds, recreates a world as bizarre and unnerving as any he wrote about in his fiction.

'Very nearly as grotesque as his fiction. The same compulsive blend of wide-eyed innocence and fascination with danger and horror' *Evening Standard*

'A non-stop demonstration of expert raconteurship' *The New York Times Book Review*

# He just wanted a decent book to read ...

Not too much to ask, is it? It was in 1935 when Allen Lane, Managing Director of Bodley Head Publishers, stood on a platform at Exeter railway station looking for something good to read on his journey back to London. His choice was limited to popular magazines and poor-quality paperbacks – the same choice faced every day by the vast majority of readers, few of whom could afford hardbacks. Lane's disappointment and subsequent anger at the range of books generally available led him to found a company – and change the world.

*'We believed in the existence in this country of a vast reading public for intelligent books at a low price, and staked everything on it'*
**Sir Allen Lane, 1902–1970, founder of Penguin Books**

The quality paperback had arrived – and not just in bookshops. Lane was adamant that his Penguins should appear in chain stores and tobacconists, and should cost no more than a packet of cigarettes.

Reading habits (and cigarette prices) have changed since 1935, but Penguin still believes in publishing the best books for everybody to enjoy. We still believe that good design costs no more than bad design, and we still believe that quality books published passionately and responsibly make the world a better place.

So wherever you see the little bird – whether it's on a piece of prize-winning literary fiction or a celebrity autobiography, political tour de force or historical masterpiece, a serial-killer thriller, reference book, world classic or a piece of pure escapism – you can bet that it represents the very best that the genre has to offer.

**Whatever you like to read – trust Penguin.**

read more
www.penguin.co.uk